The Montana Sheriff

The Montana Sheriff

A Grand, Montana Romance

Paula Altenburg

TULE
PUBLISHING

The Montana Sheriff
Copyright© 2022 Paula Altenburg
Tule Publishing First Printing, February 2022

The Tule Publishing, Inc.

First Publication by Tule Publishing 2022

Cover design by Lee Hyat Designs

ISBN: 978-1-954894-73-0

Dedication

A huge thanks goes out to Sinclair Jayne for the long-distance brainstorming session, and also to Annette Gallant, who makes every book I write stronger. She's an excellent critique partner and an even better friend.

Roxanne Snopek and Robin Bielman deserve thanks (and a medal, my firstborn, plus undying love) for laughing at me every time I say I'm going to quit writing and get a real job. The truth is, once a writer, always a writer—and they know it.

This is my second series set in Grand, Montana, a small town that came to life with the McGregors thanks to Jane Porter, Meghan Farrell, and Sinclair Jayne.

To everyone who wrote to tell me how much you liked the McGregor brothers, I hope you like the men of the Endeavour Ranch, too. Book 1 introduces Sheriff Dan McKillop, a friend of the McGregors, and Jasmine "Jazz" O'Reilly. She rides into Grand on her aging Harley-Davidson Sportster and steals his heart.

You go, girl.

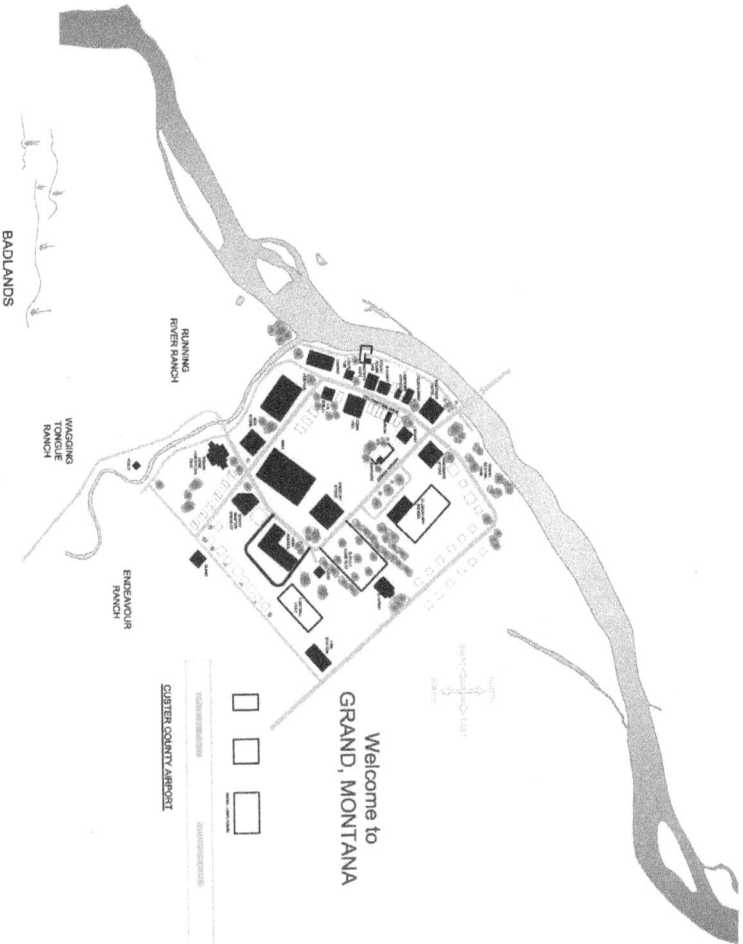

Welcome to
GRAND, MONTANA

BADLANDS

RUNNING
RIVER RANCH

WAGGING
TONGUE
RANCH

ENDEAVOUR
RANCH

CUSTER COUNTY AIRPORT

Chapter One

"LET'S SEE WHAT we've got here."

Ryan O'Connell, a tall, lean man with the rangy build of a seasoned ranch hand, bent his head over the sheets of paper on the conference room table. A careless lock of brown hair untangled itself to dangle unnoticed above a brow crinkled in concentration.

Sheriff Dan McKillop listened with mounting incredulity as his friend listed off the newly founded Endeavour Ranch's assets—115,000 acres of land, 3000 cows, 800 heifers, and 150 range bulls. That was for starters. Annual crop yields consisted of 25,000 tons of alfalfa hay and 700,000 bushels of wheat and barley. Not to mention, one hundred acres of cleared land that contained an airbase with three runways and hangar facilities.

"I still find it really hard to believe that someone bought three ranches, rolled them into one, then gifted everything to us in their will," Dallas Tucker, the third member of their trio, said.

Dallas wasn't the lone skeptic at the table. Even after three months of meetings with lawyers and accountants, Dan found it hard to believe, too. Only Ryan seemed to take it in stride—which, considering his connections, raised a number of concerns.

The three men sat in the small, windowless conference room of the Custer County Sheriff's Office located off Yellowstone Drive in the small town of Grand, Montana. Coffee dripped in the pot, tendrils of its rich aroma drifting idly on currents of warm air billowing from the room's purring heaters.

Dallas, a family doctor in Sweetheart, had driven eight hours especially for the meeting at the lawyer's office in Billings. He was bunking with Dan for a few days. Meanwhile Ryan, who'd been at loose ends since giving up a position as an operations manager for an auction and rodeo house, had flown in from Houston, Texas. Grand had three motels and he'd opted to stay alone at the one closest to what passed for downtown because he claimed Dallas snored.

They'd all been tight buddies since their undergrad days, nearly fourteen years ago now. Of the three, Dallas and Ryan had always been the risk-takers. Dan wasn't exactly risk averse—he'd raised his fair share of hell as a kid—but these days, he liked to think of himself as the calm voice of reason. While Dallas had settled down quite a bit, he wasn't as sure about Ryan.

"It's not like we're suddenly rich. There are conditions attached," Ryan reminded them. "We're required to provide search and rescue and smokejumper operations for the state, a free medical clinic, and a group home for troubled teens, all out of the proceeds. We have to live on the ranch, too. Money has been set aside for a new house—or houses, whatever we agree on—and six bunkhouses for staff."

Dan poured three cups of coffee and passed them around. The conditions were what made him less wary. It wasn't as if Ryan's estranged family members were known for philanthropy. Far from it.

But still.

"How are we supposed to meet all of those conditions and manage a ranch operation this size, too?" Dallas persisted.

Ryan's dark eyes filled with humor. "You do realize there's already staff running the Endeavour, right?"

"Are you willing to give up your family practice in Sweetheart to start over in Grand?" Dan asked Dallas.

"To live on a ranch, raise a few horses, and run my own clinic?" Dallas didn't even take time to blink. Shaggy black curls bobbed as he nodded. "Hell, yes."

Why was Dan not surprised?

"Who do you think left us the ranch?" Dallas mused.

Dan couldn't begin to imagine.

Ryan took a slow, thoughtful sip of his coffee. "Likely Judge Palmeter. Remember him?"

"Now there's a name I haven't heard in a long time." Dan rubbed the back of his neck. "I suppose anything's possible."

Judge Ian Palmeter had been presiding the day the trio had been dragged into court for stealing a police cruiser and underage drinking. A frail old man with white hair, stooped shoulders, and a gaze that could put the fear of God into an atheist, he'd delivered a blistering lecture in a deep, booming voice, asked them where they saw themselves in the future, then ordered each of them to fifty hours of community service. They found out much later that he'd also had their records cleared.

Joyriding in the police cruiser had been Ryan's idea. Back in those days he'd been pretty wild—although Dan confessed that he'd been a willing enough participant. And for his part, Dallie could be talked into anything. After a few underage drinks in a sketchy part of the city at a bar where IDs were optional, they'd seen the empty, unlocked cruiser parked in front of a convenience store. Ryan had hopped into the driver's seat and waved them both into the back.

Not one of their finer moments, true, but it had been fun while it lasted. Dan had learned his lesson, though. He was careful to keep his cruiser's keys in his pocket and the door locked no matter where it was parked, although stealing the cruiser no longer bothered him nearly as much as the drinking and driving. He came across too many DUI fatalities in his line of work to look back on their crime with any pride.

"Given the terms of the bequest, Palmeter somewhat makes sense," Dallas said. "The judge was a good man."

"We kept in touch."

"Really?" Dan and Dallas both looked at Ryan in surprise, mostly because he'd offered up a piece of personal information without them having to forcibly extract it.

Ryan shrugged his shoulders. "He looked into our prior histories. My background wasn't as pristine as yours and he was curious about it."

Not many people knew Ryan's story. He'd told them a little about it—just enough for them to fill in the blanks. He and his mother had moved to Montana from Chicago when he was six or seven. There'd been a name change involved, a lot of secretiveness, and a vague reference to a family mob connection that Dan suspected Ryan wasn't as uncertain about as he pretended. In fact, if Dan were to put money down, he'd bet that Ryan and his mother had entered the witness protection program. That was why he and Dallie never asked too many questions.

And why they were a tad skeptical about the source of their windfall now. Ryan's Chicago connections weren't the type to let go of family.

Ryan nudged the paperwork with one finger. "So. In a nutshell... We find ourselves the new owners of a ranch roughly the size of a third-world country, with obligations to set up search-and-rescue operations—that's your baby, by the way, Dan—also a medical clinic and a group home. We have a year to get ourselves situated. After that, penalties start kicking in.

"It's February right now. Calving season starts soon, but I can keep an eye on ranch business for us. We'll have to get a jump on housing soon, too. The bunkhouses might be a bigger priority than the ranch house, although we'll need to think about our own living arrangements."

Dan's head was already busy. While the US Forest Service oversaw smokejumper operations, the ranch would have to house their summer staff and any volunteers, plus provide equipment, aircraft, and space for training. Local forest service staff would need to be trained in search and rescue too, although those operations fell under the county sheriff's responsibilities—who happened to be him.

He wasn't sure how he was going to juggle being sheriff, help oversee the ranch, and get search and rescue and smokejumper operations up and running before wildfire season began, which was April.

For the first time in weeks, he felt a surge of excitement.

"There go our love lives," Dallas said cheerfully.

And...

There went the surge, plunging straight to the soles of Dan's boots. Andy had been dead for five months, yet every once in a while, at unexpected moments like this, he'd get the wind pummeled out of him all over again.

The last time he'd seen her, she'd been dancing on a tabletop and knocking back shooters at Lou's Pub, a few days before her deployment. There'd been crowd surfing involved too, because Andy never did anything halfway. A weapons expert and sharpshooter, she was killed during a skirmish in Djibouti, a small country on the Horn of Africa. Dan had no idea why she'd been there. He only knew she wasn't coming back.

And he was royally pissed about it. They'd been pals since they'd started kindergarten together. They'd lost their virginity together, too—at far too young an age. He'd hoped for something more permanent between them once she grew out of her wild streak, but deep down, he'd always known it would never happen, because "wild" didn't begin to describe her. She'd been more like a weapon of mass self-destruction—dating older men when she was a teen, giving bi-curiousness a whirl...

None of that bothered Dan. The deal breaker for him was her joining the army. He had nothing against a woman wanting to serve her country. Wild, impetuous Andy, however, never content to sit still for long, hadn't cared one bit about serving the good old US of A. She fed off adrenaline, always in search of the next thrill. Unfortunately, whatever she'd been searching for in the military, she hadn't found it.

Then again, maybe she had.

"Yoo-hoo. Danny boy. You in there?" Dallas waved a hand in front of his face.

Both of his friends were watching him as if they sensed something was off. Dan didn't want to have to explain his complicated feelings about Andy to them.

"I'm trying to figure out who we can hire to get those bunkhouses built," he said, which wasn't a lie. He dug his car keys out of his uniform pocket. "What say we take a drive out to the Endeavour and see where they should go?"

✳

JASMINE "JAZZ" O'REILLY loved nothing more than these first few chaotic seconds of freefall. She flung her arms wide and tilted her weightless body, turning into a self-propelled glider, and breathed in the sweet, cool air rushing past her as her heart pumped blood through her veins.

Then, far too soon, her parachute snapped to attention. The brilliant blue sky became silent and calm as she floated to earth, using the chute's toggles to steer her toward the tiny speck of landing site drawing closer below her. Seconds before impact, experience kicked in. She tightened her grip on the toggles, checked her alignment with the wind, fixed her gaze ahead at a forty-five-degree angle, and brought her knees and feet together.

Her feet hit the dirt. With hands, arms, elbows, and chin tucked into her chest, she stumbled forward a few steps, but managed to stay upright. The bright orange and yellow parachute gently collapsed off to one side. Not bad for her first jump of the season.

The trainer assessing her performance concurred.

"Excellent, Jazz," he said, nodding approval.

The next few hours of refresher training passed in a blur. She'd arrived at the Missoula airport a few days ago after finishing her final shift as a firefighter in Helena. This was her eighth year as a smokejumper. Word had it she was about to be offered a base manager position and she was beyond excited.

Until she found out where the base was located.

"I don't understand," Jazz said. She was seated in her base manager's office in the US Forest Service Aerial Fire Depot at Missoula International Airport. "I thought it was Rory's position that was coming open." Rory was the base manager at McCall Airport in Idaho—one of the major smokejumper training sites in the country.

"Rory's sticking around for another two years," Will, Missoula's base manager, said. "The national program manager asked me for a recommendation for Grand and I gave him your name."

Jazz wished she could feel flattered, but she knew what was going on. The average age for smokejumpers was thirty-five. Women tended to tap out well before that and she was now thirty. Will planned to foist her off on this new tiny outpost—run by cowboys, no less—while one of the male teammates she'd trained with for years got the prime posting. McCall would never be hers.

You're the one who chose a male-dominated industry so you could work outdoors. You knew what you were getting into.

She had. And she'd never once regretted it until this very

second.

Will watched her, his eyes kind. "It's not what you're thinking."

Right. "What am I thinking?"

"That I'm giving you a crap promotion because it's easier work for a woman of your advancing years."

Jazz had to smile. She liked Will. Most days. "It's as if you're psychic."

"Not psychic, but I know you." He scrubbed a hand over the stubble on his head, which he shaved to hide the beginnings of male-pattern baldness. He was forty-one years old and a smokejumper veteran. He'd been her boss for four years. "I recommended you because you're young and could use more management experience before you try and go after McCall. The competition will be fierce. This position in Grand is the perfect opportunity for you to show what you can do. I might know you're more than just one of the prettiest faces on my team, but now you get to prove it to the higher-ups."

She let that sink in. Will wasn't trying to edge her out in favor of one of the boys. He was doing her a favor. Some of the disappointment curdling her stomach disappeared. "What do you mean, *one* of the prettiest?"

"Please, Tinkerbell. You're cute, sure. But Wayne and Jay can both give you a run for your money."

Her smile loosened into a laugh. They could, indeed. Wayne looked like a Viking. He'd done some modeling in college and the other team members like to remind him of it. Jay was into bodybuilding. His face wasn't quite as handsome as Wayne's, and he was a lot stockier, but his picture had appeared in a number of sports magazines. In certain circles, he was quite famous.

Jazz, on the other hand...

The guys called her Tinkerbell, not because she was tiny—in fact, she was five ten—but because of her blond, pixie-cut hair, blue eyes, and baby face. She still got IDed in bars.

"Look at this another way," Will went on. "You'll be in charge. You won't have to put up with the new guys hitting on you, anymore."

"They don't hit on me." Not for long, anyway. A few new recruits sometimes tried to impress her at first, but lost interest when they found out she could keep up—and that she was ten years older than they thought.

She paid more attention as Will filled her in. The base in Grand, Montana, was brand new. So new in fact, it was a surprise the Forest Service had gotten it operational so quickly.

"Word has it a local guy with a crap ton of money to write off as a tax deduction footed the bill," he said when she asked how the miraculous feat was accomplished. "What do you say, Jazz? Do you want the position?"

She could only imagine the mess she'd be walking into. A whole crew would have to be hired, including a materials handler to look after the firefighting gear. But it would be a step toward her real goal, which was McCall.

"I do want it. Thank you for the recommendation. It means a lot."

She grabbed dinner with the rest of the team before settling into her bunk with the most entertaining of the three books she had on the go. A few pages in, just when the story was getting good, her phone, set to silent, vibrated. The screen lit up.

She checked the number and sighed as she answered. "Hey, Mom. What's up?"

"Hi, Jasmine." Only her mother ever called her by her full name. Her voice, soft and anxious, filled Jazz with dread. "Have you heard from Todd lately?"

Jazz closed her eyes. She was eight years older than her brother. When he was a little boy, she'd been more of a mother to him than a sister. She was tired of bailing him out of trouble. She was equally tired of their mother expecting her to. Old habits, however, died hard.

"What's he done this time?"

"I didn't ask," her mother admitted. "He called from the police station and asked me to come post his bail. What do I do?"

You call your daughter and ask her for the money. Same as always.

Jazz longed to say it, but didn't. Her mother was an aging former showgirl who couldn't name her children's

12

fathers. That they were three different men, Jazz didn't doubt. Her mother had been irresponsible for as long as she could remember.

"Do you know how much the bail is?" she asked.

There was a brief silence on the other end of the connection. She could almost see her mother doing the calculations in her head. "Two thousand."

Which meant bail was really only a thousand, because her mother couldn't resist skimming some off the top for herself. Still, the amount was large enough to suggest Todd had violated the restraining order his ex-girlfriend had taken out against him. He needed to grow up and move on.

She was tempted to tell her mother to approach a bail bonds company for the cash, but if Todd skipped out on his court date, which was a distinct possibility, Jazz would have to repay it. Either way, this phone call was going to cost her money she'd never see again. "I'll send you an e-transfer."

Her mother made a pretense of being grateful, but the call lasted only a few minutes after that. She never asked Jazz how she was doing, or even where she was.

Jazz tossed the now-silent phone aside. She'd once watched a few reruns of the TV series *Shameless*, but quit because it reminded her too much of her childhood. The biggest differences were that she'd had two brothers to care for and she'd grown up in Las Vegas. She left home when she was eighteen and never looked back, so her sense of family wasn't strong, either. She did, however, send grocery money.

And, occasionally, bail money for Todd. Thankfully her youngest brother, Leo, had managed to stay out of trouble so far. She called both of her brothers for birthdays and Christmas, trying to lessen the guilt she felt over abandoning them, but figured she'd inherited her mother and unknown father's stellar parenting DNA, because the biggest emotion she'd felt when she left them behind was relief.

She tried to go back to her book, but thanks to the call from her mother, the story had lost much of its charm. Sleep was out, too. She could switch to a less riveting book on world economies, but if it did put her out, she'd have to reread it on principle. She'd barely finished high school, and she hated sounding ignorant when the team got together, so she read a lot to compensate.

She slid from her bunk, and with her boots in her hand, tiptoed from the room. A few lights were still on but most of the others were sleeping. She wore sweats to bed when staying on base, but she stopped at her locker for her jacket, leather pants, and helmet. Then, she made her way to the parking lot. It was quiet outside. Except for the occasional plane, traffic was light around the airport at night.

Her bike was an aging Harley-Davidson Sportster 883L. She'd bought it used a few years ago after a months-long search and she loved it beyond belief. The racing green fuel tank and low mileage were what finalized the deal.

She tucked her fringe of blond bangs under the lip of her

helmet so her hair wouldn't get in her eyes, then dropped the visor over her face. Within minutes she was on the I-90 with the wind tugging at the sleeves of her jacket.

A long bike ride was second only to those few brief heartbeats of freefall for putting her world back to rights.

Chapter Two

J AZZ NAVIGATED HER Harley off the back road and onto the wide drive, passing under an arched sign that read *Endeavour Ranch*, proof the gas station attendant in Grand hadn't steered her wrong despite what she'd half begun to suspect. The five miles she'd ridden outside of town had revealed nothing but plowed fields ready for planting and heavy equipment churning up dirt.

It was a little past ten in the morning. She'd left civilization behind an hour or so ago. She drove another mile up the long, snaking drive before spotting any signs of human habitation. She cut her engine in front of a massive L-shaped, single-story mansion with three identical wings— two facing the drive and one angled to the right so it over-looked the shining waters of the Tongue River. No landscaping had yet been accomplished, although a sectioned-off piece of dry ground surrounding the walkway, and a hose with a sprinkler, indicated it might have been seeded.

The house appeared to be mostly framed in, unfinished, and uninhabited. Two half-ton trucks wearing construction company logos plastered to the doors lent credibility to her theory it was a work in progress. So did the sounds of hammering and the buzzing of saws. The Custer County sheriff's SUV next to the trucks, however, left her wondering if this was also the scene of some crime.

Behind the main house, three barns trailed the length of what remained of the drive, which reached its conclusion in front of an enormous, fenced-in pasture containing horses and an adjoining corral. The warm spring air reeked of horses, manure, raw wood, and fresh sawdust. To Jazz, who'd grown up in a large city filled with nightlife and tourists, the combination was oddly exotic, and more pleasant than not.

She scanned the wide, rolling fields that stretched to either horizon, interrupted by a lone butte far to the right. Where had they hidden the airfield?

A sudden urge to turn around and head back to Helena hit hard. She was a city girl. She knew firefighting, not ranching, and while no one hoped they'd see fires, if she didn't, what would she do with herself for a whole summer here?

She'd whip the Endeavour smokejumper operation into shape—that was what. She'd come too far to have second thoughts.

She flipped down the bike's kickstand with her right boot, then unfastened the chin strap on her helmet and swung her leg over the seat so she could stand. She hung the helmet from the handlebar and finger-combed her short hair, even though only optimism suggested it would do any good.

She'd been told to ask for Dan McKillop, one of the Endeavour's three owners. Since she didn't see anyone standing around outside to ask, she followed the sounds of construction. The day was warm so she left her leather jacket behind with her helmet. As she crossed the yard, the sun bit through her thin cotton blouse and heated the leather encasing her thighs. The protective leather biking pants were jeans-style, so they weren't super-tight, but leather didn't breathe.

She knocked on the doorframe, which seemed silly considering no door had yet been installed, but politeness overruled. She stepped past the threshold and out of the sun and waited for her eyesight to adjust.

"Anyone home?" she called out.

The hum of the saws carried on, but the hammering stopped. A head and one drywall-dusted shoulder popped sideways through an interior doorframe, as if their owner were leaning back from some task rather than allowing himself to be completely disengaged. Whatever he wrestled with appeared to be winning. Any second now, Jazz expected him to topple onto his back.

"How can I help you?" the floating head asked.

"I'm looking for Dan McKillop."

"That would be me. Give me two seconds. I'll be right with you." The head and shoulder disappeared. The hammering picked up again, with greater determination than before. Then came a grunt of what might be satisfaction, the rattle of metal on concrete, and the entire person appeared from behind the far side of the wall, wiping his hands on his jeans.

Jazz had grown up around the casinos in Vegas, so she was familiar with men who had money—or more specifically, and of far more value, the subtler nuances between those who pretended to have it and those who pretended they didn't—but, while she hadn't known what to expect a billionaire rancher on his home turf to look like, this wasn't it.

In his early to mid-thirties, Dan McKillop was a good half a head taller than her, making him at least six feet two inches, although broad shoulders gave him the appearance of far greater size. Sun-streaked blond hair, cropped short over the ears, had been licked off his forehead on top. His drywall-speckled jeans sagged off his hips beneath the tail of a T-shirt that might once have been white. Not any longer. It had a tear in one sleeve and a collar that sagged from too many washings. His steel-toed boots, covered in a fine, gray-powdered dust, showed a level of wear and tear beyond what one might expect from one of the Endeavour Ranch's wealthy new owners.

He wore an easy confidence that belonged on a much older man. It said he had no need to pretend a thing. He didn't miss anything, either. Sky-blue eyes scrutinized her in a way that said he'd memorized every detail about her, from the leather pants right down to the pale pink hue of a bra that her cotton blouse didn't quite hide, within seconds. His eyes held a question, plus a glitter of interest Jazz had seen too many times before.

Dan McKillop liked women. And he was confident women liked him.

She realized she was staring. Of course she was. His confidence regarding women wasn't misplaced.

"I'm Jazz O'Reilly," she said, stepping forward to shake his hand. He had a nice grip, firm, but not overlong. "I thought you'd be older," she blurted out, afraid he might think her stare meant she was hitting on him.

Why wouldn't he think that? He looked like a short-haired Keith Urban and had money. Women probably threw themselves at him every day.

Well, Jazz wouldn't be one of them. Men with money were nothing but trouble for women without it. She could thank the casinos and her mother for that particular life lesson.

He let go of her hand. The smile threatening the corners of his mouth stiffened before it had a chance to fully engage. The interest in his eyes flickered out of existence. "I assumed from your name that you'd be a man, so it turns out we've both been surprised. I'm going to have to rethink the sleeping arrangements at the base."

She hadn't considered he might not know she was a woman. Firefighting communities were tight-knit and she was one of a very small number of women in an already small pool of smokejumpers. Everyone knew everyone else, or at the very least, knew of them.

She swallowed a fresh wave of homesickness. She hadn't realized how much she'd come to rely on the people she worked with—both in Helena and Missoula—or how sheltered from real life she'd become, which was beyond ridiculous. She was a grown woman who leaped from airplanes without a second thought. She fought forest fires. And she ran into burning buildings—not from them.

"Whatever arrangements you have in place will be fine. I'm used to bunking with men," she said, and yes, she knew how that sounded. It wasn't the first time she'd had to deliver that line. She braced for the inevitable joke, but it never came.

"We'll find a way to make do for now. Everything is a little chaotic around here," Dan confessed, his expression rueful. His gaze flitted around the unfinished room with its sawhorses, stacks of lumber, and exposed sheetrock. "Luckily, the airfield was already in place before we took ownership of the ranch, and we've started to upgrade the three hangars, although the sleeping quarters are still a bit tight. The beds are wedged together and there's no real kitchen installed yet. There's a portable outhouse for a toilet and we've rigged up an outdoor shower with a hose. You'll have to use the laundry services in Grand until we get the plumbing sorted out." An eyebrow shot up. The smile returned. "Want to change your mind?"

He threw it down like a challenge.

She wedged her hands into her back pockets. If he was trying to get rid of her, he had another thing coming. Where she came from, what he'd just described would have sounded like heaven—not that she planned to let on. Her past was her business and she kept it to herself.

"Helping get the operation up and running was part of the job I accepted," she said. "And since I don't usually have access to indoor plumbing when I'm fighting fires, I can make do."

"Suit yourself." His eyes lit with good-natured humor. "Let's go take a look, shall we?"

✴

THE PRETTY, BLUE-EYED girl with the short, spiky blond hair and long, jagged bangs looked about as much like a firefighter as Dan did a beautician.

Not only a firefighter, but a smokejumper—one of their elite. And not only a smokejumper, but a highly recommended base manager, meaning she'd been at it a long time. He wanted to ask, "*Did they hire you when you were ten?*" Because she didn't look old enough to get into Lou's Pub, let alone smokejumper training.

But saying so might sound sexist.

She did, however, look like a Jazz. The leather pants covered mile-long, muscled legs and the short-sleeved T-shirt revealed tanned, well-toned arms. She was lean, physically fit, yet at the same time, there was a delicate freshness to her face that was decidedly female and very appealing.

And that smooth, husky voice… He could picture her with a mike on a stage in a dark, smoke-filled lounge, crooning to an appreciative crowd of drunken businessmen kicking back at the tail end of a conference.

He could imagine her equally well as a high school basketball star. She had the wholesome look down pat, too. The juxtaposition was intriguing.

What he couldn't imagine was her managing a crew of smokejumpers. Those guys ate testosterone for breakfast.

But again, saying so might sound sexist.

He dug in his jeans pocket for the keys to his SUV as he followed her into the sunshine. The only unfamiliar vehicle in the yard was a sweet little Harley-Davidson lowrider, all polished chrome and gleaming, racing-green metal. A bulky pack and full saddlebags were strapped to it. A helmet and leather jacket hung from the handlebars.

The skin on his back and upper arms shrank, as if he'd brushed up against something cold. Disquiet rippled his spine. He knew the signs of an adrenaline junkie better than most and Jazz O'Reilly was ticking the boxes. The bike might be sweet, but a lot could happen in the seven hours it took to drive from Missoula to Grand. He'd been called to three motorcycle accidents in his relatively short career as a sheriff and none had been pretty. Statistically speaking, in fatal accidents involving motorcycles and cars, cars came out the clear winners.

He had no doubt she was a competent rider. The problem was that there were a lot of other drivers on the road, and *competent* wasn't the word he'd use to describe all of them. Besides, it was hard to argue who was the better driver when you were hung up in the undercarriage of an eighteen-wheeler long haul.

It was all he could do not to deliver a lecture, as if she were some schoolkid, or one of his nieces or nephews, and not a free-thinking, legally licensed adult.

He assumed she was licensed.

"Is the bike yours?" he asked, which had to be the dumbest question he'd asked so far this week. Who else could it belong to?

"It is." Her smooth, pretty cheeks dimpled. Innocent blue eyes, unaware of his internal struggle, laughed up at him. "Is that SUV yours?"

She was quick. He'd give her that.

"Yes. Well," he amended, "technically, it belongs to the county. I'm the sheriff."

"Really?" Long, dark blond lashes fluttered. "Between construction work and ranching, when do you find the *time?*"

Now she was just plain making fun of him.

He grinned. "I never said I was good at it." He tossed the keys in his hand. "Do you want to leave the bike here and ride out with me? We can load your packs in my SUV."

The breeze ruffled that cute blond fringe of hair doing its best to hide her eyes. And failing. "How far is it to the airfield?"

"Ten miles. The road that cuts through the Endeavour from this side is dirt and not all that great."

The fun in her eyes changed to surprise. "How big is this ranch, anyway?"

It still embarrassed him to say. They'd all been so busy trying to get paperwork in order, and projects up and running, that it was hard to think of themselves as the Endeavour's owners. Most days, Dan felt more like its indentured servant.

"About 180 square miles."

Her long lashes flickered again as she processed the information. "Then I'd better take my bike to the airfield. It saves me making a second trip."

She was right, of course. It made no sense for her to leave her bike here.

"Don't you have to run every day, anyway?" he asked, straight-faced. Smokejumpers—firefighters in general—were required to stay physically fit.

She picked up her helmet and settled it on her head, fastening the strap under her chin. Her response was equally serious, although her expressive eyes danced as she spoke. "I don't normally run in leather. It chafes, especially on a hot day."

He'd always had a weakness for women, but it had been a long time since he'd met one as interesting as this. She was cute and had a good sense of humor. She reminded him of…

Damn it.

He had a type—he knew it—and Jazz O'Reilly was ticking those boxes, too. With any luck, she'd have a boyfriend. A husband. A significant other. Maybe all three. Thank God, the Endeavour, Custer County, and the state of Montana that he didn't have the free time to find out, because for the sake of his sanity, the next woman he pursued was going to be the homebody type.

He turned away. At least she wore a helmet, which wasn't legally required in the state of Montana. She got points for that. "You'll have to follow me. Stay back, though. It's been dry and you'll be eating dust, otherwise."

He drove the whole way in second gear, monitoring his rearview mirror to keep her in sight. A few miles from the ranch, he turned down a dirt road. The sign on the left pronounced it Custer County Airport.

The signage was somewhat ambitious, however. The airfield had three runways, which would allow for general aviation services, but its facilities had been sadly neglected. Nothing but private airplanes owned by locals had been serviced here in more than a decade.

The dirt road extended another five miles. He hadn't worried too much about its condition until now. He winced at the thought of how much improvements to it might cost.

It was fine for Ryan to say the money was there for him to use, but Dan couldn't quite wrap his head around an unlimited budget. If they wanted to preserve the intent of the Endeavour's bequest—that it be used for public service—then they had to be practical. Paving a dirt road because the new base manager rode a Harley wasn't enough to justify the expense. Besides, the road on the far side of the airfield that led into Grand—the one the local volunteer firefighters used—was already paved and maintained by the county.

The airfield sat on the edge of the flat, grassy plain before badlands began. One side had been completely fenced off to keep free-range cattle away. The other side had been seeded in alfalfa. A soft carpet of green already blanketed the wakening fields.

Dan pulled up next to a hangar that had been remodeled into a firefighter base station. Jazz parked beside him. He could find no fault with her driving, but then, how could he? He'd driven so slow even his grandfather would have gotten impatient and passed him.

She swung one long leg off the bike, her attention sweeping the tarmac that fronted the building. A government plane, complete with pilot, was due to arrive at the end of the month and aerial surveys would begin.

He got out of his SUV and leaned on the hood. "Let me show you around."

The interior of the steel-fabricated hangar was cool compared to the outside warmth of the day. He showed her the office with its computer and desk, the ready room, then the para-cargo bay. Jazz quickly went through the bills of lading for the boxes of equipment that had already arrived and were stored against one wall of the bay.

"I'll need to hire a materials handler," she said, and returned the clipboard to its hook by the office door.

Dan already had a few candidates in mind. "I can take care of that."

Obviously preoccupied with business, she didn't so much as spare him a look. "Thanks, but I'd prefer to take care of it myself. I need to know I can trust the person I put in charge of our safety gear." Her attention shifted to the loft and catwalk above them. "The sleeping quarters are up there?"

He could find no fault with her professionalism. She'd been focused one hundred percent on the base and the safety equipment the smokejumpers required since they'd walked into the hangar. Some of his disquiet eased. So she drove a Harley. So what?

They climbed the set of stairs at the far end of the bay. Six bunks had been crammed into a room at the top of the stairs. The two smokejumpers assigned to the base for the summer were men she likely already knew, given the size of the smokejumper pool. But then there was the pilot, who'd be on rotation, the new materials handler, and a local volunteer—also on rotation.

"You sure you're okay with these sleeping arrangements?" Dan couldn't keep from asking, even though he was beginning to sound like her mother.

"It's usually the guys' wives and girlfriends who have complaints. But at the end of the day, we all have to trust each other if we're going to work as a team." The sparkle returned to Jazz's cheerleader smile. "Besides, I'm pretty particular about who I let pack my parachute."

Had she just made a sexual reference?

Dan couldn't be sure. He did, however, hear the echo of another woman's voice in her words, and it gave him chills. Andy had been liberal when it came to sleeping arrangements, too.

Not that he could cast stones.

"Suit yourself," he said.

He didn't bring up the next problem, which was that she'd be all alone out here until the two seasonal smoke-jumpers arrived, because he'd simply assign a deputy to monitor the airfield at night until then. He wasn't doing it because the tiny, misnamed town of Grand, Montana, was a hotbed of crime. It was just that one could never be sure who the crazies might be, or where they'd turn up. His stint as sheriff had opened his eyes.

The room next to the sleeping quarters had been converted into a small kitchenette with a refrigerator, two hotplates, a sink with a portable dishwasher, and partially-stocked cupboards. After that, the tour of the smokejumper base was pretty much over.

"Call the number on the fridge and the supermarket in

Grand will deliver whatever groceries you need. They'll bill it to our account," he said. If she had any concerns about what she'd seen so far, he couldn't tell.

"What's in the other hangars?" she asked.

"Nothing, yet."

Her eyes lit up. "Can I make use of one of them?"

"I suppose," he said slowly, wary about the sudden leap of enthusiasm. "What for?"

"Physical training, which—as you pointed out—is a requirement. Plus, the hours can be long when there aren't any fires. An obstacle course would help pass the time."

It was a reasonable request. He couldn't see any harm. "Go ahead and make up a list of what you'll need. I'll give it to Ryan, one of my partners. He handles our funding."

She looked somewhat stunned. "Just like that?"

"Pretty much," Dan said. He found it hard to believe too, but it was true. "Let's go take a look at the hangars and see which one is in the best shape."

Once Jazz had picked the one to use for her obstacle course, and Dan helped carry her packs upstairs to the bunkroom, there wasn't anything more left to say.

He looked at the empty beds. He thought about the tiny kitchenette with its stock of canned goods. And he thought about this pretty girl, who looked like a cross between a prom queen and an Amazon warrior, out here all by herself, with no source of entertainment her first night.

Guilt pinched him. If she'd been the man he'd expected,

he'd invite her out for a few beers and get to know her.

"I've got to head back to the ranch and wait for a load of concrete to arrive," he said. According to the clock above the office door, it was already twenty past twelve. "You're on your own for lunch, I'm afraid. There's plenty of food in the kitchen. But how about if I pick you up around seven and take you to dinner?"

She smiled at him with those amazing blue eyes from under that long fringe of blond, jagged bangs. His heartrate, among other things, kicked up a notch, because damn it all, he had a thing for blue-eyed blonds, too.

Why not get to know her a little?

"Thanks, but I already have plans," she said.

Chapter Three

"TELL US AGAIN how the hot new base manager blew you off," Dallas said. "That story will never get old."

The three friends were having a late dinner in Lou's Pub, a favorite spot for the locals. Rumor had it that two Irish brothers, the original founders of Grand, used to bootleg their homemade whiskey to the army from the building back in the mid-1800s. The pub was dark, it had game tables set up at the back of the room where old men played chess during the day, as well as a dartboard that was currently in use by a couple of twenty-somethings who had nothing better to do with their evening. It smelled of stale beer, chewing tobacco, and horses, with a hint of pine-scented air freshener thrown in to keep the ladies happy.

Dan didn't know why he'd even bothered mentioning Jazz to his friends. It had to be the masochist in him, because it wasn't as if they were going to help boost his self-esteem. "I didn't ask her out. I invited her to dinner so we could discuss base operations and because she's alone out at the airfield. Besides, what makes you think she's hot?"

Dallas smirked and took a chug of his beer. "The invitation to dinner. So, is she?"

Definitely. And, eventually, they'd find that out for themselves. Dan didn't need to make it easy for them, though.

"Hell no. She's yellow-toothed, tattooed, and built like a linebacker. She has a face like a horse."

Ryan carefully selected a french fry off his plate and dredged it through a puddle of ketchup. "You tried to impress her and it backfired on you, huh? Face it, Dan. You're losing your touch."

He had to agree. He couldn't say for certain what he'd done to put her off, but clearly, he'd done something, because after a seven-hour drive from Missoula to a tiny backwater most people had never heard of, she couldn't possibly "already have plans."

"It's more like she was so wowed by my charm she couldn't trust herself to behave professionally around me. Luckily for you two, you don't know what it's like to have women throw themselves at you. It's a curse." He sighed. "Ah, well. Regardless of what she looks like, or how attracted she is to me, I'm going to have to spend money fixing the base up a bit more. She can't be using the same facilities as the men for the whole season."

"Why not?" Dallas asked. He took a bite of his burger, closing his eyes with a blissful expression.

Dallas was the definite free spirit of the group. He'd earned his way through medical school as a stripper and his dance moves were killer. He believed in live and let live. If something felt right, it should be done. And yet he was practical to the core.

"Because she's a woman," Dan said.

Dallas swallowed his mouthful of food. "So? She chose her career. It's not like there's a ladies' room set aside for her use when she's fighting forest fires."

"See? That attitude right there is why women don't throw themselves at you. Just because there's no ladies' room in the bushes doesn't mean she can't have one at the station. Since we own the airfield, we should at least make sure the facilities are comfortable."

"You weren't too worried about it until a woman showed up."

"Dallie's right," Ryan agreed, jumping in and nodding sagely. "You were the one who said we should focus on getting the base functional and worry about the little things later." He selected another fry from his plate. "Maybe someone warned her about your reputation for 'charm.'"

Dan's eye twitched. He conceded he might have a bit of a reputation around Grand, but in all fairness, he made it clear upfront to the women he dated that he wasn't interested in anything more than fun. Besides, since he and his friends had taken on the Endeavour, dating had become one more chore and he was usually too tired to put in the required effort.

Before he could come up with a witty response, the front

door opened and no further comment was needed.

"That can't be the new base manager," Dallas said to Ryan. "She's not yellow-toothed, horse-faced, or built like a linebacker, although I'd be happy to take a closer look to check for any tattoos."

"Mercy," Ryan said.

Dan had his back to the door so he turned to see who had come in.

The heavy wooden door swung shut behind Jazz. She paused to check out the near-empty pub. She wore her leather jacket and carried her motorcycle helmet under her arm, but she'd switched to jeans and boots. If anything, the tight jeans made her legs look even longer. Her bright blond hair shone beneath the dim backdrop of emergency lighting over the door.

Mercy, indeed. Dan rubbed his twitchy eye.

Her gaze swept the room and settled on him. A faint flush crept up her throat. The situation struck Dan as funny. Dining at Lou's alone must be her "other plans," because unless she was here to play darts, there was no one else for her to meet up with.

He really had made quite the impression on her.

There was only one cure for awkward, and that was to deal with it head-on. He half-rose and raised an arm to flag her over. "Jazz," he called out, nice and friendly. "Would you care to join us?"

"Great strategy," Dallas whispered through the smile on

his lips. "Makes it hard for her to give you the brush-off a second time. There are witnesses and now she's forced to be polite."

"Ha-ha," Dan muttered from the side of his mouth. He was trying to mend a wrong impression, not turn it to rights.

Jazz made the slow walk to their table, her steps lacking enthusiasm, and he was sorry he'd asked her to join them. He should have let her pick a table, then gone over to say hello and left her alone, because he got the strong sense it was what she would have preferred.

He tried to think of what he might have done to offend her. There'd been a few off-hand remarks about thinking she'd be a man. Had that been what did it?

Whatever it was, damage control now posed a challenge.

And Dan had never met a challenge he could refuse.

*

JAZZ SPOTTED DAN the moment she walked through the door. Lou's Pub was mostly empty and he and his handsome companions were hard for a woman to miss.

She'd chosen Lou's partly because the clerk at the grocery store swore it had the best food in town for its price range. The other determining factor had been her assumption its price range would be beneath that of a billionaire. She hoped the clerk had been right about the food, at least.

Dan waved for her to join him and she could hardly refuse, despite the sting of embarrassment flushing her skin. She should have said she wanted to get settled in at the base when he invited her to dinner, not that she had other plans, but she'd never expected to be called on a tiny white lie by the man who currently served as her boss.

The three men stood as she arrived at their table.

"Guys, this is Jazz O'Reilly, our new base manager," Dan said. He held out a chair for her, then once they were all seated, introduced his companions to her.

Jazz, a people-watcher by nature, sat quietly while the men talked. She'd been curious about the Endeavour's new owners, thanks to her deep-rooted suspicions of anyone with money—particularly those who tried to hide it—but Montana news reports had supplied very little information about them. An internet search had led back to a private holding company. A few discreet questions at the grocery store had led her to the conclusion that the locals were going to be tight-lipped about them. What little she'd picked up had come from Will—and that was Dan's name. If their choice of hangouts was any indication, they preferred anonymity.

She studied them now.

Fortune certainly favored the bold and black-haired, hazel-eyed Dallas Tucker was as bold as they came. He'd been put on this earth to have fun. If her mother were here, she'd be hitting on him for sure. He gave off a vibe that said he adored women of all age, shape, or size, and was confident they adored him in return, but his flirting was so incredibly outrageous, no one could ever mistake his attentions as serious. Jazz liked him at once, probably because of his openness. Any woman brave enough to hook up with him would have to be supremely self-confident, however, not to mention rich in her own right, so she could meet him on equal terms.

Quiet Ryan O'Connell was a tougher man to define. He had medium-brown hair and enigmatic, chocolatey-brown eyes that for some reason, made her think of kicked puppies. He seemed content to let Dan and Dallas do the talking. Yet of the three of them, if she'd met them in Vegas, he was the one she'd have sworn came from money. She couldn't quite figure him out, but the edge to him made him someone she'd be equally sure to avoid. No good ever came from the mysterious type, no matter how much—or little—money they had. The three dots tattooed on the web between the thumb and forefinger of his right hand were another red flag, as were the silvery scars on his pinkie. The former suggested he'd spent time in prison. The latter said he'd blood-sworn loyalty to some gang, although the scars looked really old, meaning he'd likely been little more than a kid if he had. She'd known men like Ryan while she was growing up, when they'd still been boys. A few had turned their lives around. Others had not.

And then there was Dan McKillop. He had the whole affable, regular-guy routine down pat. Men like Dan liked to pretend their wealth didn't matter, but they cared about image. They didn't simply write checks—they got involved in the charitable activities they supported. They got their hands dirty helping with the construction work on their own mansions too, or wrangling the breed stock on their pure-bred horse ranches along with the hired hands, always secure in the knowledge they could take that three-week vacation in Tahiti whenever they liked. Even his job as sheriff was little more than a popularity contest disguised as public service. Jazz had no patience for the Dan McKillops of the world, no matter how much they looked like Keith Urban.

Because money did matter. She doled out enough of it to her family to know that for a fact.

Dan signaled the server. "Jazz, what can I get you?"

"Iced tea, thanks."

The server was a young brunette with big brown eyes and a long, high ponytail with purple stripes worked throughout. She carried her empty tray tucked under her arm. Her smile was big and bright, and punctuated by dimples that screamed *"Let's be best friends"* to the world. That smile could put her through college on tips alone. She beamed it at Dan.

"Leila, darlin'," he said. "This is Jazz. You'll probably be seeing a lot of her. She's in charge of smoke jumping operations out at the airfield this summer. Leila is Lou's daughter," he added, speaking to Jazz.

"Smoke jumping!" Leila looked far too impressed for Jazz's level of comfort. "How did you get into something like that?"

Jazz liked that her first question hadn't been how a woman managed to qualify. "I'm a firefighter most of the year, so it was a natural progression."

"Well, welcome to Grand." Leila passed her a menu. "I recommend any of our burgers. The buns are homemade and we use local beef." The dimples reappeared. "Although if Dan's paying, order the steak. It's even better. I'll be back in a moment with your iced tea."

She walked away, her hips and ponytail swaying.

"What made smoke jumping a natural progression from firefighting?" Dallas asked Jazz, curious hazel eyes fixed on hers. "And why firefighting to begin with?"

She could hardly lead off with *I didn't know what to do with my life and the guy I was sleeping with after I landed in Helena happened to be a firefighter.* Besides, there was so much more to the story. She'd had to get her high school equivalency first, then pass all the written tests and the physical. She'd done all of those things on her own, while waiting on tables, and it had been hard, but so worth it in the end.

"A friend bet me I couldn't pass the physical so I decided to prove him wrong." She played with the menu. "Honestly, jumping out of a plane for the first time almost ended my career. I've never been so scared in my life. By the third jump though, I was hooked. I couldn't imagine anything better than those first few seconds of freefall, but then my first forest fire was the icing on the cake. It's like standing next to the railway tracks when the Amtrak goes by. The rush is incredible." She shook herself. Simply talking about it had her heart racing.

They were all staring at her.

Dallas was nodding. "Adrenaline. The reaction starts in the amygdala, then a signal is sent to the hypothalamus, which triggers the sympathetic nervous system. The autonomic nerves carry the signal to the adrenal medulla, which releases adrenaline into the bloodstream. A lot of smoke-jumpers are junkies, the same as anyone who regularly engages in extreme sports. It's better than sex."

She certainly liked the adrenaline rush, true, although she wouldn't go so far as to say she was a junkie. She wasn't sure she agreed it was better than sex, either.

Dan wore a strange look on his face. "If you're wondering about the inappropriate geek-speak, Dallie's a doctor. We're building him a clinic close to the airfield. He'll be heading the medical training for the base's volunteers and any refresher training your team might need. Unfortunately, he lacks any filters and we don't have a human resources department to tell him what comments he should keep to himself."

A doctor. Jazz realigned her initial impression of Dallas to incorporate this fresh detail, making it fit.

"Do you all have careers aside from the ranch?" she asked.

"Not me," Ryan said, glancing up from his plate. "I'm a

ranch hand at the Endeavour full time."

"But his goal is to open a group home for teenagers," Dan added.

"I need to atone for a misspent youth," Ryan confirmed. "I liked fancy cars."

"You liked stealing fancy cars. There's a difference." Dan tapped the table. He had strong, long-fingered, work-roughened hands. "Jazz needs money to set up a training obstacle course in one of the empty hangars."

The reformed car thief—if that story was true—was in charge of their operating budget? Jazz longed to know why.

Ryan settled his napkin on top of his now-empty plate. "Tell me more."

She explained what she had in mind while she sipped the iced tea Leila brought her.

His eyes lit up. "Can anyone use it?"

"You're paying for it, so I don't see why not." She accepted the enormous burger Leila set in front of her with a smile. "All I'd ask is that you check the schedule ahead of time in case the firefighters have it booked for training."

"Done." He spoke to Dan. "I'll add the money to your revised budget for washroom facilities at the base."

"We're getting new washrooms?" Jazz looked at Dan, too. There were better things to be spending the base's budget on.

"I meant to talk to you about that."

Dallas coughed into his fist. He skidded his chair away

from the table. "Come on, Light-fingered Louie," he said to Ryan. "I have a shift at the hospital first thing in the morning and I need a ride home. I hear there's a sheriff's vehicle parked on the street. We can boost that."

"Stay away from my car," Dan warned them. Jazz couldn't swear that his alarm was unfeigned.

The two men left. Jazz and Dan were now alone in the pub. The dart players were long gone and Leila was wiping down tables and chairs.

"You don't have to stay on my account," she said. "I'm used to eating alone."

His eyes crinkled at the corners as his lips shifted into a grin. "That's okay. My evening is free. I didn't already have plans."

Heat crept up her neck and spread to her cheeks. Fair skin was a curse. It was on the tip of her tongue to make up some excuse for why she'd lied, but that was what had gotten her in trouble in the first place. She took a large bite of her burger, which was fantastic—as Leila had promised—to save herself from digging in any deeper.

"I apologize if Dallas's comments about adrenaline and sex offended you," Dan continued. "He has a tendency to say whatever he's thinking."

Jazz tried to think why that comment might be considered offensive, or why Dan seemed to assume she'd be offended by it, and came up with nothing. She swallowed her food and met his gaze.

And forgot what she'd been thinking about. His eyes were so *blue*. So inviting. So friendly.

Adrenaline and sex.

That was what she'd been thinking about. And now, with those blue eyes fastened on her, she couldn't unthink it. She'd thought Ryan was the dangerous one in the trio. She'd been mistaken.

"It takes a lot more than an offhand remark about sex to offend me," she said.

"Yet I can't help but feel that this afternoon, I crossed some line I'm not aware of." The blue eyes remained friendly enough, but were now a great deal more watchful and probing. Dan the Sheriff must be awesome when it came to interrogation. "What does offend you?"

Jazz examined her half-empty plate. Her appetite was healthy. She burned a lot of calories in the run of a day thanks to training, and yet, no matter how good it was, there was no way she could eat all this food.

She couldn't avoid giving him an answer, either. She might as well be honest.

"I've always made it a rule not to become involved with my coworkers," she said. "While I know your invitation to dinner was intended to be polite, I try to avoid situations that might be misconstrued. Having dinner with my boss is one of those situations."

"I guess I can understand that." His gaze became less intense, as if her answer satisfied any concerns he might have.

"Especially since you're now the boss of men who'd be your former peers."

"Exactly." She was relieved he understood.

She was equally glad he had no idea what she'd really been thinking. Dan McKillop, with his billion-dollar eyes and hot, country music star manners and looks, was a dangerous man, and despite knowing better, she found him attractive—meaning she was no different than thousands of women.

She'd do well to avoid him as much as she could.

Chapter Four

DAN PARKED HIS car in the lot next to the hangar. The cooling engine ticked in the morning heat as he got out. He didn't have to go to the office today, so he thought he'd check in on base operations before heading to the construction site at the ranch.

Thank God they only had two more weeks until their new house would be ready for occupation. He'd dreaded the thought of picking out furniture, and considered asking his mother for help, but Ryan had taken the bull by the horns—so to speak—and hired an interior decorator for the three separate units. That interview with the decorator had been brutal. Who knew there could be so many different types and colors of backsplashes and so many places to put them?

Gravel crunched under his boots. Alfalfa swayed in the fields bordering the airfield. Spring had been dry and the crop would be ready for the first cut in a few weeks. The stems would soon blossom, and bright purple heads would speckle the wide swath of green.

He rounded the end of the long, metal-clad building and strode toward the main doors with purpose. He had a second motive for coming here this morning at this early hour, one that had nothing to do with alfalfa. Jazz had dodged him for the better part of a month. The few times he'd dropped by the base, she'd been too busy to talk. That ended today. He understood why she didn't want to be seen fraternizing with her boss, even if he'd gotten the distinct impression that wasn't the whole truth behind her reluctance. For some reason, she just plain disliked him.

That was too bad for her. They had to communicate through more than the weekly email reports she copied him on.

For example, he was dying to see the new obstacle course Ryan was raving about, as well as the new washroom facilities. They'd come out of his operating budget, after all. And it bugged him that Ryan had authorized so much money. Worried him, too. Yes, they had an enormous net worth between them. Their income didn't come from any one single source, however. It was wrapped up in investments in various businesses, and as one of those businesses, the Endeavour remained its own entity. They couldn't take from one to pay off the debts of another, and right now, between the new house, the airfield, and the clinic, the Endeavour was racking up bills. He and Dallas had finally dug in their heels and told Ryan if he wanted a private helicopter so he could travel the whole ranch in one day, he could fund it himself.

Dan had slept a lot better at night when he was poor.

He pushed on the strike panel of the hangar's steel door. Its smooth metal was already warm from the sun. Cooler air hit him inside.

The base was a far different place than it had been a month ago. Bright fluorescent lighting ran the length of the building. The materials handler Jazz hired had been installed in an office, and the inventory piled haphazard along one wall had been sorted, packed, and the packs stored until ready for use. She'd done a great job.

Dan followed the aroma of coffee. Jazz had turned another empty office into a conference/breakroom so visitors didn't have to go upstairs to the small kitchenette.

He found her leaning against one wall of the breakroom with a mug in her hand, her back to him. She wore black track shorts that showed a long length of tanned leg, and a plain white tank top with a black sports bra underneath. The damp tank top stuck to her skin. Equally damp, spikey blond hair was another clue that she'd just returned from a run. He had a mental flash of her naked, and heat licked from his gut to his groin. Inappropriate?

Yes and no. He didn't really consider himself her boss, because at the end of the day she didn't answer to him, but she obviously thought of him that way, and he was in a position of power, so he conceded the rules likely did apply. Since only he knew what he was thinking, however, what the hell.

She was talking to Eli, the new materials handler, and

Brody, one of the volunteer firemen from Grand. Brody had obviously come from a run, too, and it was very likely they'd been running together.

Annoyance nudged Dan. Jazz considered having dinner with him to be crossing a line, and yet an early morning run with a married man who worked for her was okay. He wondered what the man's wife might have to say about that.

"Good morning," Eli said when he caught sight of Dan in the doorway. "You're up early."

"I think you guys have me beat."

Jazz twisted around at the sound of his voice and looked at him over her shoulder. Her cheeks, flushed from exertion, brought out the intense blue of her eyes. A narrow barrette clipped her long fringe of bangs off her face. She wore a too-bright, pretty much fake, friendly smile on her lips, and looked so energetic, so full of life, and reminded him so much of *Andy*, that Dan had to catch himself before he said something foolish. Tension built at the back of his head, cramping the muscles in his neck and shoulders.

He admitted it. He wasn't here to improve communications between them because of the base. He was here because he was attracted to her. Because she was his type. And maybe, deep down, he was here because he wanted proof that his type were all disasters. Once he had confirmation of it, he could finally give up on this unhealthy obsession with strong-willed women.

Because that was all this was—an obsession. He'd had

unfinished business with Andy and his subconscious must have transferred his need to complete it onto Jazz, a woman who reminded him of her. The tension cramping his neck muscles eased. Acknowledging the problem was the first step to solving it. There was that small matter of her disliking him, too. That was one more challenge he chose to accept.

He was a great guy, damn it.

"I've got the day off and thought I'd take a look at this new obstacle course. It's all Ryan's been talking about," he said.

"You're in luck. That's up next, right after coffee," Jazz replied.

Dan considered himself fairly athletic, but her morning workout consisted of a long-distance run and then an obstacle course?

This, he had to see.

Eli offered Dan a cup of coffee too, which he accepted. He tried to keep his mind on the conversation and not Jazz's damp tank top while he sipped it.

Then, he walked across the tarmac with Jazz, followed by Brody.

"My goal is to beat Jazz's best time," Brody said, bouncing on his toes. "I remain hopeful."

"Good luck. You're going to need it," Jazz replied, cheerful.

Dan gaped when they entered the hangar. The floor of the building had been completely transformed. Where there once had been nothing but concrete and steel a complex, colorful obstacle course, all bright pinks, blues, and yellows, had sprouted like weeds. The course sprawled from one end to the other, and towered in places. Thick mats padded the floor—not that they'd do any good. What appeared to be a simulated helicopter fuselage took up the far wall, from the ground to the ceiling some fifty feet above. Jazz had been busy.

"I have to complete a safety inspection before we can start, so I'll walk you around the course first," she said.

There were ten obstacles in all. She checked every rope and flat surface for fraying and dirt as she explained each obstacle to him. It was clear she took safety seriously and Dan was impressed.

"This is where we practice how to safely exit a helicopter," she said when they reached the far wall.

The helicopter fuselage could only be accessed by a zipline from above or the knotted rope dangling from the platform to the ground. She scaled the rope with a cat's predatory grace, the muscles on her upper arms and shoulders flexing and bunching, her feet catching the knots and boosting her upward. She made it look easy. Dan knew it wasn't. She did a quick check of the platform's surface, then descended to the floor with breathtaking speed.

"All set," she announced, wiping her palms on her shorts.

They returned to the start of the course. Brody, who'd been patiently waiting for them, shrugged into a jumpsuit, then lifted a pack hanging from the wall and slipped his arms through the straps.

Jazz held up a second suit. "Full gear or for fun?" she inquired of Dan.

He eyed the suit and the packs. Those packs were filled with firefighting equipment and weighed more than a hundred pounds each. She couldn't be serious. "Which are you doing?"

"Full gear. But I've already been around the course once, so I'm not going to try to break my own record," she added, speaking to Brody.

If she'd be running the course carrying close to her own body weight, then Dan wasn't taking the easy way out. "Full gear it is."

"Turn around, Jazz," Brody said. "The boss is going to have to strip down to the tighty-whities, first."

Dan shucked his work shirt and jeans and Brody helped him suit up.

He eyed the first obstacle. It was a rope bridge, stretched across twenty feet of matting. According to Brody, he had to cling to it upside down, using his arms and legs, and shimmy across—with the heavy pack weighing him down.

He could do this. But only if he made a few concessions.

"You'd better go first," he said to Brody, "because I doubt if I'll be breaking anyone's record."

"If you make it to the halfway point, I'm going to be really impressed," Brody replied. His grin widened. "I might even vote for you in the next election, Sheriff."

While Dan might not break any records, and the equipment he carried was heavy as hell, not making it all the way to the end was no longer an option. "Whatever, funny man."

"Since I'm not trying to break any records either, I'll bring up the rear," Jazz said, looking all perky and fresh. "There are a few rules. The helicopter exit is for the smoke-jumpers, so it's not part of the course. Don't attempt it. Only one person on an obstacle at a time. And if you can't complete an obstacle on the second try, you're finished."

"No pressure," Dan muttered.

A tiny frown puckered her brow. "You can have a third try, if you like. Since this is your first run," she offered. "And you aren't a firefighter."

"Thanks."

Great. Now Dan was going to have to do the entire course without any errors at all. It wasn't because he was worried about having a woman out-perform him...

Then again, maybe it was. He wasn't the one carrying his own weight in equipment, after all. And he really wanted to improve her opinion of him.

He made it across the rope bridge, crawled under horizontal cargo netting using his elbows to drag him along, and scaled the vertical net, before he began to slow down.

He wiped the sweat from his forehead on his sleeve. The jumpsuit was heat-protected to withstand 2000 degrees. That couldn't possibly include the inside of the suit, because he could swear it had already passed the 1000-degree mark. Brody was already well in the lead. Meanwhile, Jazz was doing a great job of hiding her impatience behind him—all of which forced him to examine his pride.

And yet his pride demanded he soldier on.

He powered through the tire obstacle, leaping from one to the other, then grimly swung across the monkey bars with his stomach clawing its way into his chest. He was breathing heavily now, but he'd seen a defibrillator on the wall so figured he should be fine. Jazz and Brody were both first responders, and if things did reach that point, he'd have to live with the shame. Or die from it. He was good with that, too.

He sneaked a peek at Jazz. She looked bored.

He took a running start and cleared the next wall. Thank God he was tall. By now Brody was finished with the course and had jogged back to help cheer him on.

"Go, Dan. You got this," he said.

Dan hoped the guy burned in hell. One of his lungs had already collapsed and the other had sprung a slow leak. He had to ask himself who he was still trying to impress, because if it was Jazz, that ship had sailed at least two obstacles back.

No, now he was in this for himself. What he lacked in speed he made up for in endurance. He'd already passed the halfway point without using his two tries. After today though, he planned on taking up running again. He wasn't as fit as he'd thought.

The next two obstacles were easier and gave his scorched lungs a bit of a break. He ran across the balance beam, then ended the course with a stump hop that was more of a limp. He longed to pass out on the mats, but Brody was already pounding his back and offering congratulations, so dying was out of the question.

Jazz sprinted past him in a dash for the knotted rope, then skidded to a halt. She turned back to where he was trying to hang on to his dignity, and quite possibly, his breakfast. He caught her expression and realized she was going to quit now rather than show him up completely.

He didn't need pity. There had to be some way he could turn this into a win.

"I bet you dinner that you can't make it to the top of the rope with that pack on your back," he wheezed.

The slight smile on her lips said she had nothing to prove, and furthermore, wasn't falling for that. "Thanks, but I'm done for the day."

"If I'd known a free meal was on the line, I'd have climbed it," Brody said.

✳

JAZZ WONDERED WHAT the penalty was for accidentally killing her boss, who also happened to be the county sheriff, because Dan looked like he might die.

She shouldn't have given him the option of wearing full

gear when she knew he hadn't spent the necessary hours working out. She and Brody had gone through weeks of training before they'd suited up and run the entire course, and halfway through, when it became obvious he wasn't going to quit, she'd felt mean. At least he'd had the common sense to slow down and take his time rather than charge full speed ahead, trying to keep pace with Brody.

Even so, his face was alarmingly red.

"Let's get out of these suits and go grab some breakfast," she said. "Are you hungry?"

"Starved."

He was likely lying, because he sported a few classic symptoms of overexertion and hunger wasn't among them. The red face suggested his blood pressure was higher than usual—although thankfully his breathing, while irregular, was already returning to normal, so by the time they got to the kitchenette, assuming he didn't collapse first, he should be okay. A sports drink filled with electrolytes would do him wonders. She'd monitor him until convinced he'd survive.

Once their practice gear was properly stored, they crossed the tarmac in search of breakfast. The team on active duty had already finished eating and the kitchenette was empty. Brody grabbed a bagel and cheese, a bottle of apple juice, and an orange from the picked-over remains of the buffet spread out on the table.

"I'm not on call this week and the day job awaits," he explained to Dan. "Gotta go."

That left her alone with Dan—something she hadn't thought through.

Her appearance, for example, was somewhat of a concern. While not particularly worried about makeup and such, she'd just run ten miles, then an obstacle course, and her hair was sticky with dried, salty sweat. Her shirt was stiff and her smell might be an issue. She'd love to grab a shower, but she couldn't do that until after Dan had been fed.

Dan, on the other hand, had gotten his second wind. His shirt and jeans were clean because he'd removed them before running the course. His short blond hair, licked up in front from where he'd run his fingers through it, looked no worse for wear. And as for his smell…

He smelled delicious. A combination of aftershave and rugged outdoorsman wafted from him. Throw in intense blue eyes that didn't miss much and he'd never need money for women to adore him. He made parts she sometimes forgot she owned tingle, and she wasn't interested in him in the least—because she knew better.

She took two sports drinks and two bottles of water from the fridge and thrust one of each at him. "Drink them both," she ordered. "The sports drink first, but you can water it down if you prefer."

Blue eyes twinkled at her. "Yes, ma'am. Can I have orange juice, too?"

He was making fun of her, and okay, yes, maybe she'd sounded a bit more dictatorial than required, since he no longer looked as if he might pass out and die. "You're welcome to whatever you want."

His eyebrows rode up.

"Within reason," she added. She was the red-faced one now, and it had nothing to do with overexertion. Why— *why*—did he always make her think about sex when he looked at her that way?

He cracked open the sports drink. "Define *reason*," he said, before chugging half of it down. His eyes never left hers. She felt the heat of that gaze the entire length of her body, from her cheeks to her toes.

And, just like that, she was free-falling.

She could play this either one of two ways—pretend she didn't know he was flirting with her, or she could address it head-on. Normally, she preferred the direct approach when it came to men in the workplace. It cleared the air. The few times it hadn't, she'd simply reverted to avoidance and toughed out the season.

Dan, however, was her boss, and so far, avoiding him had gotten her nowhere. How could it, when she'd known who'd entered the lunchroom earlier without turning around, or Eli having to say a word? It was as if she'd developed some sort of Dan radar—a sixth sense. She got a little buzz whenever she heard the sound of his voice. Standing next to him left her light-headed. Therefore, she was part of the problem.

A big part.

Because yes, Dan was hot. Yes, she found him attractive. And yes, he knew she did. But she had no plans to end up like her mother, ruined by some high-rolling rich guy in her quest for a lifestyle she longed for but couldn't earn on her own. Jazz's current lifestyle, achieved through hard work, suited her fine. If she wanted meaningless, no-strings-attached sex, she could find it with a stranger on Craigslist. It would be safer.

"Anything you've paid for is yours," she clarified for him, secure in the knowledge that, regardless of where they got their funding, her paycheck came from the US Forest Service, so she wasn't setting herself up.

Dan twisted the cap off the bottle of water. "In that case, since everyone else appears to be finished eating, I'll take sausages, hash browns, and a bagel as well as the juice, and a bunch of those grapes. I wouldn't mind a cup of coffee, either. I've got a long day ahead of me."

Forlorn purple grapes, ignored by the men in favor of the carbs on the menu, spilled out of a white plastic bowl on the table. She persisted in ordering fresh fruit even if she was the only person who ever ate it. She nudged the bowl toward him. "Help yourself."

She put on a fresh pot of coffee and dropped two slices of bread in the toaster for herself, then filled a plate with leftover hash browns and sausage and set the microwave for two minutes. She settled into a plastic chair across the table from him while she waited.

"For someone without any training, you took that course like a champ," she said, watching him as he slathered cream cheese on his bagel.

"Did you say champ or chump?"

She snagged her toast and added it to her plate. "Either way, I'm impressed."

The microwave chimed. Dan retrieved his sausage and hash browns before she could get up. "It takes a heart attack to impress you? You're a hard woman, Jazz." He ate a few bites of his bagel, then accepted the cup of coffee she poured for him. "Tell me a bit about yourself. Where did you grow up?"

Jazz didn't like telling people about her childhood. While they usually found it exciting, to her, it was normal—and in retrospect, more than a little depressing. She debated saying she'd grown up in Southern California, but she'd already gotten caught in one lie so decided on a brief response in the hopes he might take the hint.

"Vegas."

"Huh. That explains a few things."

"Oh, really? Such as…"

"You being so pretty, and yet unconventional. Let's see how good my profiling skills are… Your mom was a show-girl. Your dad owns a casino and you're rebelling against entering the family business. You wound up in Montana because you're fascinated by cowboys—we're notoriously honest and upstanding. How am I doing so far?"

The light tone of his voice and the way his eyes crinkled around the edges told her he was teasing, so she answered in kind. It didn't matter whether or not what she said was the truth. He didn't really expect her to tell him her life story.

"Exemplary, Sheriff. But a bit off the mark." She held up her fingers and began ticking off his observations. "Yes, my mom was a showgirl. Sorry, I have no idea who my dad was or if there's any family business to rebel against. My mother used to take me to the world finals for professional bull riders every year when I was little, which was where we both developed a fascination for cowboys." That was how she'd found out what a buckle bunny was, too, and probably explained where the oldest of her little brothers came from, because while Jazz might be pretty, back then, her mother had been stunningly, breathtakingly beautiful. She still was, in fact. "'Honest and upstanding' had nothing to do with it. Those guys were buff. And sorry, but I wound up in Montana because that was how far the only bus ticket I could afford went, not because of its plethora of cowboys."

That last bit of information came out way too intense. She'd thought she'd come to terms with her family issues. Apparently not.

The grin in Dan's eyes faded. "I—"

The fire alarm rang, interrupting, and whatever he'd been about to say was lost.

Chapter Five

J AZZ PUSHED HER half-empty plate to one side.

"I've got to double-check the guys' gear before they head out. Go ahead and finish your breakfast. And don't forget to drink your water," she called over her shoulder as she darted out of the room.

Dan heard her issuing more orders on the catwalk outside as the base sprang to life. While staying put went against every instinct he owned, he knew better than to get in the smokejumpers' way. He'd already seen what went down in the ready room during drills and didn't need to see it again. They'd be gone in less than ten minutes, and if he really wanted to make himself useful, he could clean up the kitchenette for whoever'd pulled KP duty.

He wolfed down his second breakfast of the morning, then loaded the portable dishwasher. He cleaned up the pots and pans and wiped down the table. Since Jazz hadn't finished her breakfast, he heated a plate of leftovers and carried it downstairs.

He found her in the operations room, glued to the radio while taking notes. Her three-man crew were long gone.

She didn't look up from her task. "It was a lightning strike. The jumpers are going to clear a fire control line to contain it before it can spread."

"Eat this." He set the plate of food, napkin, and a knife and fork next to her elbow.

"Thank you." She tugged the plate toward her and stabbed a piece of sausage with the fork in her left hand while she continued to take notes with her right.

He was already late for the day's work he'd lined up at the ranch, but the wistful edge in her words held him in place. He took a stool against the wall and sat quietly where he could watch her without interrupting.

He had excellent profiling skills. He had the good-ole-boy shtick down to a science, which helped. The trick was to make his questions sound innocent and not give a suspect enough time to think. He didn't listen to what they said so much as the way they said it, or even better, what they avoided saying at all—and Jazz hadn't liked him asking about Vegas. She'd bristled a little when he'd teased her about how it explained a vague, undefined "thing" about her, too.

Then, when he threw a few stereotypes out there as bait, she'd grabbed them, just as he'd hoped, and he'd gotten a fairly clear snapshot of her early life. She had issues with her mother, who had a weakness for men. Since her mother liked bull riders in particular, he could guess where Jazz got her fearless streak from.

And when she said she'd bought a bus ticket to Montana because it was as far as she could afford to go, she hadn't been joking. Her pupils had contracted ever so slightly, she'd blinked a few extra times, and then she'd looked away, just for a split second, as if trying to hide what she was thinking.

If he'd read her right, then she'd left home with no money and quite likely on the outs with her mother—yet look where she was now. Her confidence confirmed why she'd come so highly recommended. He'd seen seasoned state troopers display nerves a whole lot less steady. He wouldn't pit one of them against her on an obstacle course, that was for sure.

To round off his observations, she missed smoke jumping. Any idiot could tell that.

When she finally glanced up, more than an hour had sped by. She rolled her shoulders, stretched her arms over her head, and as she spun around, she caught sight of him. She froze, arms extended. Surprise crossed her face. She brought her arms to her sides, to his disappointment. She had a fair bit of cleavage packed inside that black sports bra.

"I didn't realize you were still here," she said.

And again, if he paid close attention to the way she said things, it told him a lot more than words, because he'd swear in court that it wasn't him, personally, she didn't like. But she did dislike something about him. He'd swear to that, too. What could it possibly be? That he was a sheriff?

Maybe she wasn't estranged from her mother. Maybe

she'd left Vegas in a hurry because she'd been on the run from the law.

No, that was too much of a stretch. He'd go with the estranged mother, because he wasn't yet ready to admit that it really was him she had so little use for.

"I was too sore to move," he said, which was only a tiny bend of the truth. His left shoulder might never fully recover. "I made it this far and decided I'd probably pass out before I got to my car, and it's hot out there. I didn't want to die of heatstroke on the tarmac after surviving the near-fatal heart attack you gave me."

A small smile tugged at her lips. "I offered you three attempts at those obstacles but you wouldn't listen. How was I to know you have a weak heart?"

He took that small smile, and light, teasing tone, as good signs she knew he was flirting.

"Tell you what," he said. He'd made a lot of assumptions about her, which as far as investigations went were a starting point only, and he was dying to find out if he'd profiled her right. "We're having an open house at the Endeavour in a few weeks. Everyone in Grand is invited, including you and your team. You show up, stay a few hours, and we'll call it even."

That was another slight stretch of the truth. He and the guys had talked about hosting a party and opening up the new house to the whole town, sort of a "welcome to Grand" for Dallas and Ryan, but while Dallas had loved the idea,

Ryan, who shied away from attention like a horse from a snake, had distanced himself from the discussions.

Dan, too, had been slow to fully commit because his sisters were going to go nuts. So far, Allie and Kirstin had minded their own business when it came to the ranch, but they loved planning parties and there'd be no holding them back.

There'd be no holding them back if they got even a whiff that he was interested in Jazz, either. They'd show him no mercy. He shuddered to think of what they might tell her about him. He'd played around a fair bit while waiting for Andy to sort her life out and his reputation might have suffered a little.

Maybe a lot.

"I own no responsibility for your lack of physical conditioning," Jazz said. "I propose a new deal. How about you install a washer and dryer for us on the base so we don't have to take the used gear to the laundromat in town anymore, if we come to the open house?"

"I have to *bribe* you to come to a party?" He didn't miss how she'd included her team's participation as part of the deal, either. Then his brain replayed the first part of her statement. He narrowed his eyes. "You think I'm out of *shape*?"

"Focus on what's important, Sheriff," she said, neatly dodging his second question, and fair enough. By her standards, yes, he was. "We can't keep using the local laundromat to clean our gear, because then it's not always on site and mission ready. It can sometimes be a few days before we get it back."

He hadn't thought about that. She was right. It was a situation he couldn't allow to continue. They absolutely needed their PPE to be ready to go at all times.

"All you had to do was ask for them, you know," he said. "I'd have prioritized them higher."

"I'll keep that in mind. I'm not used to managing an un-limited budget." *Unlike some people*, her neutral tone implied—and they were right back to square one, with him getting the sense that he'd done or said something wrong.

Maybe he was reading criticism where none was implied. References to money, no matter how slight, always made him defensive. Too many of Grand's citizens, most of whom had known him his whole life, had felt the need to point out how it changed a person, and yet Dan didn't feel any different. He didn't throw it around as if it grew on trees, either.

He did agree with Jazz, however, that working with very few financial constraints took getting used to, which was why he was more than happy to let Ryan deal with the headache it caused. "I wouldn't say it's unlimited, exactly. Expenses that are above and beyond still have to make sense."

"You mean like the new ladies' washroom, complete with a shower and bathtub, when there's only one woman work-ing here?" Her voice was gently teasing, but this time there was no mistaking the hint of reproof in her blue eyes.

He shrugged. She might be used to roughing it when she was firefighting, but she had an office job now and there was no reason for her to be roughing it every day. He knew the way guys talked in locker rooms. He wouldn't want one of his sisters working under those conditions.

"I believe in planning ahead. Next year, yours might be an all-woman team."

"In which case a men's room would have worked just as well. The ladies' room is nice, don't get me wrong, but the expense could have been better spent on installing the men's room first. The guys have been using the ladies' room so they don't have to shower outside anymore, anyway."

He scrubbed his brow with his thumb. He was developing a real hate for money. Who knew spending it—or not—could be such a big deal? "Most people would just say thank you and let it go."

Jazz's cheeks colored. "Thank you."

The way she blushed was the one anomaly about her he couldn't quite figure out. It didn't fit.

"Do you miss smoke jumping?" he asked, even though he already knew that she did. He hoped the off-topic question might catch her off guard enough that he'd get a genuine response.

She shot him a lopsided smile. "Every time the alarm rings."

"Then why give it up?"

"Because as a woman, my shelf life as a smokejumper is only about industry average. I'd rather give it up on my own terms than be forced out by a bad back or damaged knees, or worse, patriarchy. At least as a base manager I can still take part in operations. Besides, I have my job in Helena to return to at the end of every season, so I haven't given up firefighting entirely, and I can always go skydiving on my days off."

She had a practical outlook, which he admired, but her sense of self-preservation?

Holy crap.

His neck and shoulder muscles cramped up again. It was past time for him to leave.

"Pick out the washer and dryer you want and send me the information," he said, testing his legs to make sure they'd hold him before prying his butt off the stool. "I'll need it to figure out the hookup requirements."

✳

EVEN THOUGH DAN had already installed the new washer and dryer, a deal was a deal and he'd upheld his end of the bargain.

By the time Jazz arrived at the Endeavour Ranch for the open house, the yard was packed with vehicles and the house was bursting with people. A large crowd had gathered on the lawn at the side of the house closest to her, its attention focused on something she couldn't see. A steady buzz of voices drifted across the yard.

Heads turned to stare as she squeezed her motorcycle into a tiny space next to the garage. She'd already figured out she was the only woman in Grand who owned a bike—or at least, one of very few—and while she didn't think her panties were showing, by the looks on some people's faces, she couldn't be sure.

She took another quick chance on exposing them as she dismounted, then smoothed the short skirt of her dress to make sure it hadn't hiked up in back. She rarely got to dress like a girl during the summer smoke jumping months, so, since the ranch wasn't far from the base, she'd abandoned her usual leather bike gear and helmet and dug out the one sundress she owned. She'd put on makeup and painted her toenails too, although sadly, she'd only packed flip-flops, not pretty sandals. She could only carry so much in her saddle-bags.

She'd had to come alone because it turned out she was the only one at the base who worried about keeping a deal with the boss. One team member wanted to FaceTime with his wife and daughters. Three others remained on call and were packing equipment. One had simply refused. *"He provides the facilities, Jazz. I don't care what he thinks. My job doesn't depend on him. If this base closed, I'd be moved to a different one. Besides, I already get free food and I'm allergic to horses."*

As a base manager, with more competition for her position, Jazz's employment options were no longer as secure as a jumper's, so when it came to workplace politics, she told herself she should play along. Dan's friendly blue eyes, and the warm smile that made her lose track of time, not to mention the way he paid attention to her when she spoke as if he really cared about her opinions, had nothing to do with her being here.

Nothing at all.

She'd make a quick stop, find him and say hello as proof she'd held up her end of the bargain, then be on her way.

The spectators had lost interest in her. Whatever was happening at the front of the crowd held far more appeal to them than either her or her panties, to her relief. She wasn't shy, but she'd been so focused on her career for the past twelve years that her social circle had grown very small, pretty much limited to fellow firefighters and their partners.

Also, small-town Montana was beyond her comprehension. The people, while nice, were astoundingly nosy. She couldn't figure out whether they were really interested in her or simply being polite. Up until Grand, no one in her life had given a damn what she did.

Dallas Tucker poked his head from the half-open side garage door, scaring the crap out of her, and she jumped. He shot a furtive glance left, then right, then beckoned to her.

"Quick, come inside before anyone sees us," he said.

She'd gotten to know Dallas a little better over the past

few weeks when he'd given her team their refresher medical training. Everyone liked him. He was personable, funny, and didn't take himself too seriously, and yet when it mattered, he was all business. Curious to find out why he was hiding when this was his party too, she obliged him and stepped into the garage. He shut the door behind her, then flipped the lock.

Calling this a garage was like calling the White House a cottage. There might as well be a posted sign in here proclaiming "Money to Burn." Panels fitted into the structured steel roof filled the interior with plenty of natural light. The concrete floor had been finished with a textured industrial paint, then sealed with a high-gloss epoxy. Two bay doors challenged the front of the building. A heavy-duty, wood and steel workbench propped up the far wall. Dozens of what appeared to be gently used tools hung on hooks above it.

She counted five cars, all fast and high end. While she was no expert on luxury vehicles, she did like speed and it seemed someone at the ranch might be a collector. The likeliest bet would be Ryan, who'd admitted to having a taste for them.

"Is something wrong?" she asked Dallas.

"Kind of." He dug his fingers through his dark mop of curls and scrunched up one side of his face, managing to look both innocent and guilty at once, like one of her little brothers, caught stealing candy. "A reporter from some sort of lifestyle magazine showed up, wanting to do an interview with the three of us. I said I'd go find Ryan. Now she's got Dan cornered at the side of the house."

So that was what the crowd was about.

"And you couldn't find him?" she guessed, still confused as to why he was hiding out in the garage.

"Who, Ryan?" Dallas waved a hand. "He took off long before people started to arrive. He hates this sort of thing."

She got it now. "You left Dan to fend for himself, didn't you?"

"Of course, I did. I don't need my private life splashed all over the internet and he's already a public figure. Besides, he's used to grilling people for information. Let him see how the other side feels for a change. But now I feel kind of bad about throwing him under the bus. Would you go rescue him for me?"

He had to be kidding. "And how am I supposed to do that?"

He thrust a phone into her hand. "Pretend to be his assistant. Hand him this and say he's got an important phone call that can't wait."

Jazz tried to hand the phone back. "Isn't there anyone else who can do it?"

"Are you kidding me? Did you see the size of that crowd? They all know him. And so far, not one person has stepped up to the plate. They're all too busy watching him squirm. They might like him well enough as a person, but at the end of the day, no one loves the law. Especially when the law is stinking rich." Dallas's eyes danced. "I don't plan to remind anyone that I'm also stinking rich. I have to live here, too. You, on the other hand, are only going to be here for a few months."

True enough. Plus, she'd been interviewed for a so-called lifestyle magazine before and it hadn't been fun. Not in the least. The reporter had only been interested in the negative aspects of being a woman smokejumper—he'd grilled her about things like workplace sexual harassment—and hadn't cared at all for what made it the best job in the world. As a result, she no longer granted interviews.

Dan might want to consider adopting her policy.

"I'll do it, but I'm doing it for him, not you," she said. She tried to sound severe. "You should be ashamed of yourself."

"Oh, I am," Dallas assured her.

He sounded anything but.

Poor Dan.

She grabbed Dallas's hand and slapped his phone into his palm. "I don't need this."

She left him hiding in the garage and crossed the paved drive. She ended up next to a lovely woman with long, curling dark hair, smooth, almond-colored skin, and striking, periwinkle-blue eyes standing at the back of the crowd. She carried a sleeping baby in her arms. She looked vaguely familiar, but Jazz couldn't place her.

"I can't watch any longer. Dan thinks he's holding his own, but Adriana Gallant is toying with him," the woman said with a wince. She had a faint accent that Jazz couldn't place either. She cradled the baby with one arm and held out her free hand. "I'm Mara McGregor. You must be the smokejumper everyone's talking about."

Jazz shook her hand. "Jazz O'Reilly. I'm not a jumper anymore, I'm afraid. I'm the base's summer manager." A tiny lump formed in her throat. That was tougher to say than she'd expected.

It must have showed. Sympathy and understanding flooded Mara's eyes. "It's hard seeing others doing something you love, isn't it?"

"It is," Jazz agreed.

"Don't worry, it will get easier. And you'll love it in Grand. The people are wonderful." Mara shifted the baby so its head rested against her shoulder. "It's nice to meet you, Jazz. I hope I run into you again, but right now, I've got to go find my husband. He has to work this afternoon, so we can't stay." She crinkled her nose, her smile rueful. "Besides, I've been interviewed by Adriana before and I don't really want to draw her attention to me."

With that ambiguous statement, Mara departed.

It was the graceful way she moved her whole body, as well as the flow of her dark curls as she walked away, that triggered Jazz's memory as to why she looked so familiar. Mara McGregor had to be Mara Ramos, a former professional dancer featured in music videos for Little Zee, an up-and-coming pop star. She'd been all over the news a few years ago when she'd broken her leg in a skiing accident. Jazz remembered only because she'd liked the video for one of Little Zee's songs. Little Zee himself seemed like a bit of a douche.

Mara really would know how it felt to sit on the sidelines. She appeared to be content with her life now, though, so Jazz hoped things had worked out for the best. She seemed very nice.

Right now, Jazz was curious to see why Mara could no longer stomach watching a reporter toying with Dan. Everyone else seemed to be enjoying themselves.

Adriana Gallant, accompanied by a young male cameraman, had him cornered against the side of the house. Pretty in an even-featured, generic way that no doubt suited television, and slathered in a thick layer of makeup, she appeared to be in her early forties but striving for a revival of thirty.

"Is it true that you inherited your wealth from a former judge?" she was asking.

Jazz hadn't heard that particular rumor, not that she'd paid much attention. She'd assumed Dan and his two billionaire buddies had been born into wealth and only recently gained access to trust funds, because sometimes, people expected their heirs to learn how the other half lived before giving them money to throw about.

"I have no comment on that." Dan lifted a hand to shade his eyes. Sunlight glinted off his casually combed hair. The gesture drew Adriana's attention to the solid muscles of his chest and upper arms. Cougar eyes lingered a little too long.

The whole scene irritated Jazz to no end. What bugged her the most was the way he smiled at the reporter—as if every word she spoke was pure gold. He was no doubt well aware of the impression he made on women. She saw no point in staging a rescue when he was doing just fine on his own.

Then she caught the twitch of a muscle at the hinge of his jaw. It suggested he was wired maybe a little too tight and his calm demeanor took more effort to hold than he let on.

Adriana shifted a few flirty inches closer to him and fired off her next question. "I understand that philanthropy is a condition of your inheritance. You and your partners must have some interesting connections. Who was the last person you called?"

Dan flashed that easy smile of his—the one so full of charming, down-home sincerity it made a woman's toes curl. He'd tried it on Jazz more than once.

Jazz, however, was under no illusions as to its true purpose, at least right at this moment. He was trying hard to deflect.

"My mother," he said.

Adriana's own smile sharpened. "I do believe you're being evasive, Sheriff McKillop. What are you hiding?"

"Nothing but the dirty pots and pans in my oven, ma'am," he replied promptly. "The dishwasher was full and I had company coming."

"Tell me a little about the Endeavour's co-owners." Adriana scanned the crowd, then paused for effect. Any second now, her gloves would come off. "Are they hiding in your oven with those pots and pans?"

Dan, either oblivious or uncaring as to what was about to go down, kept right on with the wise answers that would only heighten a reporter's curiosity, not curb it. He clearly wasn't used to this type of interview—this wasn't a crime scene.

Not yet.

"Oh, I don't think so," he said.

"I met Dr. Tucker briefly before he disappeared." Adriana made a show of checking her notes. "I understand he's one of your partners. He's from Sweetheart, correct?" She didn't wait for Dan's confirmation before moving on. "There's very little information about your third partner, however. Ryan O'Connell. What might his background be?"

And there it was. The *thing* Dan was doing his best to avoid. Jazz felt it. So did the crowd.

Adriana felt it, too. The scent of blood had her quivering. Not much wonder Mara had fled. Seeing him squirm gave Jazz no pleasure either. She couldn't stand by and watch. He was going to owe her a lot more than a washer and dryer for this though.

She shouldered her way through the front line of onlookers and popped free of the crowd. She edged up beside him and touched his arm.

"Pardon me, Sheriff," she murmured. "There's a small"—she cleared her throat and left a slight but meaningful pause—"*matter* that requires your attention."

Blue eyes swiveled to her. A glimmer of hope sparked in their depths.

Then he asked, "Can it wait?"

Chapter Six

CAN IT WAIT.

He'd actually said that to her. He'd felt his lips moving.

But Adriana Gallant was digging for dirt on the ranch and its owners and his goal right now was to deflect her. Ryan had warned them the press would show up today, but Dallie and Dan, both new to money and not understanding what the fuss was about, had laughed off the idea. This was Montana. There were other, and larger, ranch operations. Why would anyone care about theirs?

The answer, of course, was they didn't. The real story had to be Ryan. While Adriana might know his name, an internet search would have netted her nothing. His past was a tightly sealed secret. And that would have been enough to bring out the bloodhound in her.

But telling Adriana flat out that their third partner was none of her business would be like pouring gasoline on himself and striking a match. When Mara Ramos McGregor first came to Grand, she'd been as down on her luck as it was possible to get and yet Adriana hadn't shown her one ounce of compassion. Dan had been trying to decide how best to let her know the interview was over without making things worse when Jazz, with her bright blond, pixie-cut hair and long, athletic limbs, parted the crowd and burst forth like an angel, and his train of thought bounced off the tracks. She'd offered him the perfect escape.

A little too perfect.

He had no clue as to what had inspired her to come to his rescue. He sincerely hoped it wasn't because he'd reeked of the desperation he'd felt. If so, he'd be the butt of Grand's jokes until something better came along, and since not much ever happened here, that could take months. They were good people but they took their entertainment where they could find it.

Unreadable eyes fixed on his.

"No. It can't," Jazz murmured. She sounded calm enough, but it could be a front. With women, one never knew.

"Thank you, Jazz. I'm sorry, Ms. Gallant," he said to the other woman, "but I'm going to have to put an end to our interview."

The reporter, however, had already picked up on a new angle for her story and wasn't about to let it fly by.

"Jazz... What an interesting name. And who might you be?" she inquired.

"My girlfriend," Dan interjected, at the exact same time Jazz said, "An employee." The cameraman got an up-close shot of Jazz's start of surprise.

Adriana looked at Dan. Her eyebrows hiked into her hairline. "Would you two like to take a moment and discuss it?"

"She's both," Dan said.

"Really?" Adriana took in Jazz's simple dress and flip-flops in a way that spoke louder than words. "Do you have a last name, honey?"

Dan's insides shifted location. If a woman had scrutinized Andy in that manner, and then called her *honey* in that tone of voice, their body would never be found. All Jazz said was "Yes," and left it at that.

But her cheeks had gone pink, so she was rattled, and he didn't like it. If Adriana was trying to insinuate that she lacked the money and style a billionaire's girlfriend would require, she was way off the mark. The truth was, Jazz looked fresh and pretty and, honestly, way out of his league.

He debated telling Adriana that Jazz was a smokejumper and shift the interview over to her—because, come on, that was a far more impressive story than three guys who'd been handed money—but to paraphrase a line from *Guardians of the Galaxy*, he might be an asshole but he wasn't a one-hundred-percent dick. It was time to get them both the heck out of Dodge.

"Thank you for coming all the way to Grand to check out the Endeavour Ranch," he said to Adriana and her cameraman, who was beginning to look slightly less bored.

"You're welcome to stay for the entertainment, but right now, you'll have to excuse us."

He placed a hand on Jazz's back and nudged her toward the house. His fingers spanned her narrow waist and soaked up the heat of her skin through her dress. The crowd parted for them. His hand remained on the small of her back as he propelled her around the corner of the house. He nodded and spoke a few words to anyone who greeted him along the way.

He didn't, however, slow down until they were through the front door. He needed a private space to decompress.

The Endeavour's main building was really three houses in one. The central area was communal space. It held a lounge for entertaining, a large office occupied mostly by Ryan, and a washroom for guests. A door to the left led to Ryan's private living space. Dallie's door was opposite the main entrance, through the lounge. Dan's was to his right, facing Ryan's.

He thrust his door open and propelled Jazz into his living room. The interior designer had filled it with brown leather furniture, artwork from some famous Montana painter he'd never heard of, and vases upon vases of flowers. He kind of liked it, and kind of felt overwhelmed and afraid to touch anything when he was in it. He definitely didn't dare rearrange it.

Through a partially closed, sliding barn door, he heard his mother and his sister Kirstin rustling about in a kitchen roughly the size of his entire county sheriff's office. What he was supposed to do with a kitchen that size he had no idea. Maybe he'd bring his barbecue inside. Steaks, he could handle.

He didn't want to see his mother or sisters right now. They'd hardly be sympathetic and would have too many questions—mostly for Jazz. He seized her hand and dragged her into a hallway off the living room, then through another one of the incessant doors in this confounded place. He closed it behind them and leaned against it, clenching his eyelids tightly shut in relief and soaked up the peace and quiet.

The bedroom was large, but not intimidatingly so. Not like the kitchen. Patio doors filled one wall. The doors led to a private garden and sitting area where he could drink his morning coffee if he chose, or if he had time. He'd drawn the curtains closed earlier that morning so that anyone wandering the garden couldn't see in. This was the only room in the entire house that felt like his. Here, he could think.

"I just need a few minutes," he said.

Jazz maintained her silence until finally, he opened his eyes.

She'd taken possession of the comfortable armchair next to the gas fireplace at the foot of the enormous bed. He liked to sit in that chair and read at night. She'd kicked off her flip-flops and was exploring the texture of the thick gray carpet with her toes. He enjoyed the feel of that carpet, too. He was going to enjoy it even more from now on, after seeing her pleasure.

"Sorry about that," he said.

She couldn't quite hold on to a straight face. At least she'd found the humor in it. "You should be sorry. I try to bail you out and you ask me if it can *wait*? Then you release the breaking news that I'm your girlfriend?"

He had no real explanation to give her.

"I panicked," he said.

"I noticed."

"If it makes you feel any better, there's not one person in Grand who believed it."

She pressed her hands to her chest and fluttered her lashes. "Stop with the flattery. It'll go straight to my head."

"For what it's worth, that speaks to their opinion of me, not you."

"A young, single sheriff with a bad reputation... What a shocker."

"Since we're listing my attributes, you forgot about good-looking and rich," he said.

"No, I didn't." She slid her feet into her flip-flops and stood. "I'll allow that you panicked about the girlfriend thing. But what on earth possessed you to invite her to stay? Aren't you worried about the questions she'll ask people or what they might tell her about you?" She sounded curious, not judgy.

"Not in the slightest." He was a whole lot more concerned about what they'd tell Jazz. He'd just announced that she was his girlfriend, after all. Like that wouldn't come back to bite him, because there'd be more than one Good Samaritan who'd feel obliged to warn her that his track record with women wasn't spot free. "Grand is a small town and we look after our own. They'll say I'm the youngest and brightest sheriff Custer County ever had. They'll likely bring up a few stories about my wild high school days—the kind they'd joke about at a wedding. They'll tell her my favorite food, where I went to school, and that I'm good to my mother. And I asked her to stay because I didn't want her to think I was running from her."

She tilted her head in a way that said she was choosing a careful response. He couldn't wait to hear it.

"Don't take this the wrong way, but when I'm fighting a forest fire that's out of control, I don't stand my ground because I care what someone else thinks."

She had him there.

"I've got a good handle on it. I've been the sheriff in Custer County for almost three years." He'd been interviewed all of once during that time, too. Some kids had gone on a weekend camping trip and gotten lost in the badlands.

"She wasn't interviewing you about being a sheriff." The way Jazz studied his face, with such a mixture of confusion and interest, said she wasn't buying what he tried to sell. Rightly so. "Hasn't anyone ever dug into your private life, before?"

"Why would they? Until this past February, my life has pretty much been an open book. No digging required."

He'd never felt the need to explain why he sucked so badly at being rich before. Everyone in Grand already knew. But he'd never had a problem with the day-to-day pressures of being a sheriff. He enjoyed his job, in fact. When it came to the Endeavour's money, however?

It exhausted him in ways he'd never dreamed. Judge Palmeter had a cruel sense of justice.

He dropped onto the foot of the bed, settled in, and opened up. "The guys and I had a slight misunderstanding with the law our first year in college and the judge took pity on us. At least, we thought it was pity. It turns out the man was really a sadist. He left us several billion dollars and a huge swathe of Montana."

"The bastard," Jazz murmured.

She sat down beside him, bending one knee slightly so that they partially faced, which caused the short skirt of her dress to ride up her smooth thighs, and braced her hands on either side of her hips. Dan had a mental flashback to when he was fourteen and alone with a girl on a bed for the first time, and despite the air-conditioning, the room became very warm.

"Right?" he said, shaking it off. "My life was a whole lot simpler this time last year. I suppose I shouldn't complain, but money really complicates things."

"Not having it really complicates things, too."

The careful way she pointed it out wasn't offhand or joking, or even the slightest bit envious, which were the ways most of his friends and family reacted when comparing their lives to his. She simply stated a fact. He remembered she'd once spent the last of her money on a bus out of Vegas, and while her current paycheck was okay, he earned a lot more as sheriff.

The annoying trust fund was a whole other issue, but her situation made it plain he'd definitely picked the wrong audience for that particular complaint. "True enough. Forget I said anything."

"No. It's okay. I've never had billions of dollars or huge swathes of land given to me, so I have no idea what your complications might be."

Aha. Now he got it. It wasn't him she had any serious objections regarding. She disliked the fact he had money.

Dan had been middle class his whole life, so while he didn't really know what it was like to be poor, he'd never been rich before, either. As a lawman, however, he'd dealt with people on both sides of that particular fence and they each had their problems. For example, when it came to people she viewed as entitled, Jazz had a prickly stick up her butt.

What was that all about?

His mental profiling of her kicked into gear. She might have gotten to where she was in life all on her own, but she believed he'd had it easy. He couldn't say for certain what her obstacles were. He did know that his path wasn't without them.

"I can't even date anymore without wondering whether my sparkling good humor, movie-star looks, or the money is the true attraction," he sighed. "It's a curse."

A bit more of her reserve chipped away. "I didn't realize you'd only recently inherited your wealth."

"That's because I reek of money." He nodded sagely. "I dine in Grand's finest restaurant and wear the latest in Custer County Sheriff's attire. Not to mention, I interview as if I've done it my whole life."

She wanted to laugh. He could tell.

"Do you realize you have several hundred guests roaming around and not one of the ranch's owners are at the party?" she asked.

"Dallas will entertain them."

He loved Grand and its people, but being the highlight of their day had worn really thin. He needed a break. Winning Jazz over would do. Man, he longed to kiss her. Her pretty, cheerleader face, less than two feet from his, was tempting. She looked so damned sweet in a dress...

He was attracted to her in a way he hadn't been to any woman in a very long time. It was more than sexual, although there was plenty of that. She was different. Unique. Something no amount of money would ever be able to buy. The prickly reserve that hid a great sense of humor made the package complete. She'd choose a man on her own terms. What a lucky bastard he'd be, too.

Dan intended to be that lucky bastard.

"Dallas is hiding in the garage," she said.

He massaged his eyes with a thumb and forefinger. So much for luck. Since he'd planned this open house over Ryan's objections so he could get to know Jazz outside of the base, he supposed this served him right.

"Good help is so hard to find."

The corners of Jazz's mouth flickered. "He asked me to save you, so that's got to be good for at least one billion dollars."

If she only knew.

"About that small matter that requires my attention..." he said, shifting a few inches closer.

Her eyes told him she was onto his game, and she edged a few inches away. "Forget it. It can wait."

"Ha-ha. Very funny."

It kind of was—and the joke was on him. He knew how to tempt a woman like Jazz, though. Give her reason to think she might be playing with fire and she'd be all-in. He brushed the bobbed fringe of blond bangs aside with the tips of his fingers, just to gauge her reaction.

A faint intake of breath. A deepening of the blue of her eyes and a slight dip of the long lashes. But overall, it appeared she'd decided that any fire developing between them wasn't yet out of control and she was safe enough standing her ground.

He'd see about that.

He'd never been one to rush things, however. There was a lot to be said for romancing a woman and she was worth the extra effort. He might have gotten a little rusty the past few months, but he was sure it would come back.

"Since we've already violated your personal rule about not becoming involved with a coworker—and because I looked it up and there's no law against it—why not have dinner with me?"

"*We* haven't violated anything," she replied. "Because we're not involved. Saying something doesn't make it true. Besides, do you really believe I should reward you for bad behavior?"

"Maybe you're the one who'll be getting the reward." He gifted her with a grin designed to let her know what that reward was going to be, too.

Then he sat back to enjoy her response.

"I'm sure there are any number of women who'd look forward to it." The implication, of course, being that she wasn't one of them. "Tell you what," she relented. "I'll stay for your barbecue, which means we'd be having dinner together here, and you can use the time to mitigate the damage you've done to my professional reputation here in Grand."

He didn't dare celebrate yet. "Does mitigation mean I have to confess to Adriana Gallant that I jumped the gun about us?"

"Jumped the gun?" Jazz echoed. "You flat-out lied. But no," she relented. "No one with half a brain pays attention to the type of trash she reports on, anyway."

✳

BESIDES, JAZZ WOULD never give the reporter the satisfaction of being proved right. The way she'd dismissed her still stung.

As far as Dan went, however, all of her preconceived notions about him required a revision, because it turned out Sheriff McKillop wasn't a case of still waters running deep. He was exactly what he seemed on the surface—a handsome, hard-working, somewhat flirty Montana sheriff with a slow smile that made women line up for arrest and should be considered entrapment. As an added attraction, he could poke fun at himself. And while it was impossible for her to feel sorry for someone worth billions, she did feel a slight twinge of sympathy for a man so far out of his depth. Windfalls of the Endeavour's magnitude should come with a user guide for beginners.

But that wasn't her problem.

"You just insulted about three quarters of the female population in this country with that remark, but I'll take it," he said.

The room was so quiet the walls had to be soundproofed,

because no one would ever know that what appeared to her to be half of Custer County was roaming the ranch. The thick carpet was gorgeous. The platform bed was crafted from solid wood, with a full-grain, Italian leather, quilted headboard and side panels. Their combined weight barely made a dent in a sixteen-inch thick, king-sized mattress.

They looked at each other.

"I've never been in a billionaire's bedroom, before," she said. She'd never expected to end up in one either, even if all they were doing was talking.

Dan made a face. "Me either. It's my favorite room in the house, though."

"I'm sure it is."

He laughed.

"You should get back to your guests."

"I probably should."

Neither one of them moved.

She breathed in the soft, clean scent of his skin. Every sense she owned—all six of them—flipped into hyperawareness. Her heart did a fast little flip-flop she hadn't experienced since she was thirteen and an eighteen-year-old rodeo hand mistook her for sixteen.

He was going to kiss her.

And she really, really wanted him to.

No. No, she did not.

While she doubted if Dan telling some tabloid they were in a relationship would have any impact one way or the other on her long-term career, at the end of the day, he was still her boss, at least for the summer, and she wanted that position at McCall so badly she could taste it. For weeks now, she'd been doing her best to prove she could manage the largest smokejumper base in the country. She believed she'd done an above average job here in Grand, helping to get the new base operational.

So, while kissing him wouldn't necessarily be the worst mistake she'd ever make, it wouldn't be her smartest move either. She had her future to think of and no one was more invested in it than her.

"Do it and I'll file a harassment suit against you," she said, because if he wanted to play this type of game she could give as good as she got.

His lips hovered a few inches from hers. Blue eyes glittered. Both eyebrows rose. Then he sat back and the mattress jostled a little. "Since when is kissing your girlfriend considered a case for harassment?"

"Since I'm not your girlfriend."

"No? Tell that to Adriana Gallant."

He looked so smugly pleased with himself that she had to laugh, even though she was only encouraging him.

"Are you worried the guys at the base will wonder how you got the new washer and dryer?" he asked.

Yes. Absolutely. "Why should I care what they think?"

"Because apparently, your reputation requires mitigation."

"My reputation does not require mitigation. The damage done to it—by you, I might add—needs mitigating. There's a big difference."

"You just told me that, when you stand your ground at a forest fire, your actions aren't based on what someone else thinks. And yet you didn't want to have dinner with me because you try to avoid situations that might be misconstrued. I believe those were your exact words. Do you care about other people's opinions or not?"

Of course she didn't. She'd never cared what people thought—not about her mother, or her family situation, and especially not about her.

At least, not very much. Okay, maybe she did. Just a little.

"Fighting a forest fire and having dinner with you are hardly the same thing," she said.

"That's exactly what I thought," he said. "And yet I get the feeling the forest fire holds more appeal for you than I do."

"I don't know about that. In a lot of ways, you're alike." She was less likely to get burned by a forest fire, though. Heat licked through her at the promise in his eyes, proving her right.

He nodded, indicating complete understanding. "It's the way we both induce an adrenaline rush in you."

"That's not at all what I meant. I—"

The bedroom door opened.

Chapter Seven

"**D**AN? YOU IN here?"

Whoever spoke didn't wait for an answer. A woman peered around the half-opened door. Jazz pushed Dan away, tumbling him onto his back, and scrambled off the low bed. She tugged her short skirt into place, her face screaming with heat. This time, her panties had definitely been showing.

"Whoops!" the woman exclaimed. Then she quickly recovered. She glared past Jazz at Dan. "What is wrong with you, you idiot? Dallas and Ryan are missing, you have the whole county roaming the ranch—including some reporter with a cameraman—and yet you can't resist giving random women a private tour of your bedroom?"

"I take it you missed the interview on the side lawn," Dan said. "Jazz isn't just any woman. She's my girlfriend."

"You must be the smokejumper everyone is talking about," the woman said to Jazz. "I'd pictured you smarter. Not even his money makes him worth wasting your time."

Dan rolled off the bed and positioned himself next to Jazz. They looked like teenagers caught with their pants down. He slid an arm around her waist and hugged her to him. "Sweetheart, this is my oldest sister, Kirstin. Believe it or not, she loves me."

Now that he pointed the relationship out, Jazz could see the resemblance. Kirstin looked like her brother, with the same hair, eyes, and features, although Jazz guessed her to be a good decade older. She was a few inches shorter than Jazz and a few pounds heavier, mostly around the middle, but she gave the impression of a much larger woman.

Amazonian, in fact.

"Of course, I love you," Kirstin said. "You have money."

"Not you," Dan said. "I meant Jazz."

His sister pushed the door the rest of the way open and stepped into the room. "Sorry. In that case I meant to say, of course she loves you. You have money."

"You have a sister?" Jazz said to Dan, because she couldn't find anything more intelligent to contribute. She'd never considered that he might have family. Why would she? Until this afternoon, she'd done her best not to think about him in any context other than as her boss.

She should have stuck with her original instincts.

"I have two of them. They're both older and they both think they're my mother," he replied.

She pried herself free of his arm. If only her face wasn't so hot. "This isn't what it looks like."

"It probably isn't," Kirstin conceded. She looked thoughtful. An unexpected smile lit up her face, making her look even more like her brother. "Which is kind of too bad." The smile vanished as fast as it appeared. "But you have games lined up for the kids and people waiting for you to start them," she said to Dan. "So move it."

She hustled them both out of the room, then through Dan's living room—which looked like something off HGTV—and into the Endeavour's main lounge, which was currently empty.

"Go be a host," she said, before shutting the living room door in their faces.

"I feel like I just got a spanking," Jazz said. Or maybe hit by a truck.

"Is spanking something you're into?" Dan asked.

She ignored that. "Does your sister live with you?"

"Good God, no." His horror was too funny for words. "She's got eight kids, all under twelve. Two sets of twins," he explained, saving her from having to do the math. "Four and six years old. But don't let that scare you. Twins run in their father's side of the family, not ours."

"We aren't a *couple*," Jazz said, even though he was yanking her chain and she was wasting her breath. He'd found a joke and was running with it.

"We aren't? Because I'd never kiss my grandma like this."

He captured her face in his hands, bent his knees to bring him to eye level, then, in a smooth, practiced move that had her catching her breath, settled his mouth over hers. The kiss was warm, firm, and far more seductive than she'd ever have suspected, because she lost the use of her legs. Her arms took on a life of their own, winding around his neck without any instruction from her. And then, she was kissing him back.

She couldn't say for sure how it happened, but he'd lifted her into his arms and had her braced against the wall next to his door. She'd wrapped her legs around his waist and his hands were under the hem of her skirt. His fingers toyed with the dampening crotch of her panties.

He tracked the tip of his tongue along the seam of her lips, just a light, teasing touch that left her gasping for air, before pulling away. He lowered her to her feet, then straightened the skirt of her dress because it was beyond her.

They stared at each other as the seconds ticked by. Her mouth opened and closed. She could think of nothing to say. Disparate thoughts churned in her head, but none coalesced into anything lucid other than that Dan McKillop could kiss.

He looked equally stunned. He wasn't as speechless, however.

"We have two choices," he said, scrubbing his hand through his hair. "We try to make it past Kirstin and head back to my bedroom, or we put this off until later."

"A third choice would be to forget it ever happened."

"I can't do that. Can you?" The heat in his eyes said he was being honest, and he dared her to be honest, too.

"No," Jazz admitted. "But it's not something I want either," she added, since they were being so honest.

The muscle in his jaw appeared to be experiencing a seizure. She watched it with fascination.

"You could have fooled me. Care to explain?"

"I'm not interested in getting involved with anyone," she said, then pivoted toward the door, all set to make a face-saving exit.

"Hang on a sec." His hand on her arm stopped her. "I'm not going to ask you to do anything you don't want. Don't let one little kiss scare you off."

As if.

She'd been afraid plenty of times in her life and it had never stopped her, before. It was the possibility he might know what held her back when she didn't that she couldn't handle. He had a way of picking bits of information out of her, then piecing them together, that was starting to freak her out.

And also annoy her.

"You're right. It was just a little kiss," she said, hoping to annoy him a bit too, and going straight for his male ego to do it.

"I wouldn't say it was *little*." He looked mildly affronted, so it appeared she'd succeeded.

"No? I distinctly heard you refer to it as 'one little kiss.' It's okay," she said generously, because she played with fire for a living, "I happen to agree."

The thumb of the hand holding her arm rubbed circles

against the soft inside of her elbow. *Ignore it,* her stern, inner voice—the one that kept her alive—ordered. His level of self-control was far more impressive than hers. The heat in his eyes had downgraded from a boil to a light simmer in a matter of seconds.

"Why don't we try it again? For comparison's sake?" he suggested.

Much like when he'd tackled the obstacle course, it seemed Dan didn't know when to quit. Fortunately for them both, Jazz didn't suffer from the same affliction. She hadn't jumped out of an airplane that very first time without calculating the odds, and the way she tallied them now, he wouldn't stop unless she did.

There was a time and a place to accept a challenge from him, however, and although she wasn't sure when that moment might be, this wasn't it. If she let him kiss her now, she had no doubt she'd find herself on her back on the floor, right here in the lounge, where anyone could walk in and catch them, giving Adriana one heck of a story. She was amazed no one had walked in already. The public bathrooms were right next to the main entry.

While she didn't care for the idea of an audience, the possibility of getting horizontal with Dan did hold a certain appeal. Enough so, in fact, that it was becoming harder and harder to remember why it was such a bad idea. Did she really want to sleep with her boss?

Because that was where things between them were headed.

"Maybe some other time," she said, taking care to sound indifferent despite the way her heart was pounding out jumping jacks in her chest. Whether temptation or alarm drove the rush of adrenaline, she couldn't say.

"At least stick around for the barbecue this evening. It'll be fun. What do you say?"

"Why not?" she said, because the best way to avoid temptation was to play with it, of course. He'd accepted rejection a lot more easily than she'd anticipated—suspiciously, possibly disappointingly so—meaning he was most likely up to something, and she was curious.

He took her hand and twirled her around so that she faced the door, leaving her head spinning for a whole different reason. "Lead on, then. It wasn't as if we were going to make it past Kirstin, anyway," he said.

*

THE JURY WAS still out on Dan's sister—Dan too, for that matter—but his mother was lovely.

Freda McKillop introduced herself to Jazz while Dan was busy fielding good-natured congratulations on finding a woman and rounding up contestants for the junior rodeo the Endeavour's cowhands had organized. Jazz was watching him from the other side of the paddock fence. Adriana and her cameraman must have opted to cut their losses because they were nowhere to be found.

Jazz had wondered at first if everyone left Dan to hang himself because they didn't like him, or maybe they were simply jealous of his good fortune. It turned out that neither was the case. If anything, they seemed genuinely determined to help keep him real.

A tall, red-headed man with the lean hips and muscular upper body of a cowboy clapped Dan on the shoulder. "Congratulations on finally upgrading to a real woman from those fancy latex dolls that perform all the same functions."

"Thanks. I guess you'll be wanting them back," Dan replied, proving he could take a joke, and earning a few laughs from the cowhands while he was at it.

"She's a little young for you, ain't she?" someone else said.

If they were fishing to find out her age, Dan wasn't biting. "She makes up for it by being far more mature than I am."

"You planning on running for sheriff again next year?"

"Of course." Dan fitted another child-sized baseball helmet on a junior contestant's head and tightened the chin strap. "Custer County needs a good sheriff."

Jazz was familiar with men being boys, and they were trying to get a rise out of him in front of her, which wasn't likely to happen. She'd never heard of a sheep toss before, however, so that was of a great deal more interest. The group of hyperactive five-year-olds wearing helmets gathered next to the gate, and the anxious mothers hovering nearby, erased any confusion as to who'd be tossed and who'd do the tossing.

Dan's two twin sets of nieces and nephews—two four-year-old boys and two six-year-old girls—hadn't quite decided if riding sheep was their thing, and they kept him busy while they made up their minds. Anxious queries abounded and fears were successfully laid to rest.

She had to admit, his general appeal to men, women, and children alike made him that much more attractive to her, and he'd already been doing just fine. But if she started something with him, and it ended up going sideways on her, how might it affect her chances at McCall?

Freda had squeezed in between Jazz and two teenagers placing bets on how well their younger siblings would do. "Dan sent me to keep an eye on you," she said. "He seems to think you're a flight risk. Don't make me have to chase you."

Freda didn't look much like her son and daughter, other than that she and Kirstin were about the same size. With silvery-gray hair caught in a long braid, and a loose-fitting sundress that skirted her ankles, she had "hippie" written all over her. While she seemed more milk-and-cookies than dangerous, after meeting Kirstin, Jazz wasn't about to test her as to whether or not she meant what she said.

They chatted while they watched the first two riders kiss the dirt, bounce up with giant smiles on their wee faces, then run off to collect their candy reward. The teenagers eventually grew bored and moved on, leaving them temporarily alone at the rail.

Freda seized the tiny window of opportunity. "I'm so glad to see Dan finally taking an interest in a woman again," she said quietly.

Jazz reached a fairly obvious conclusion about his mother's revelation. She wasn't sure how she felt about it either, other than somewhat confused. There wasn't much about him to suggest his heart had ever been broken. Or really, jeopardized to begin with.

"How long has it been since the breakup?" she asked. She wondered if Freda understood that she and Dan weren't really a couple.

Freda looked startled, although she quickly recovered. "I see. He hasn't told you about Andy yet. Don't worry, he will." She patted Jazz's arm, evidently assuming that she might need reassurance that her love life was secure.

People moved into the vacant space at the rail and the window for privacy closed, so Jazz let it drop. She wasn't about to pump Dan's mother for personal information, particularly when she wasn't really entitled to it.

But she wanted to know.

A mind-numbing assortment of his family, friends, and acquaintances kept her entertained the rest of the day, mostly with stories of Dan. A lot of them were somewhat off-color, but there was enough upselling of his finer qualities going on that she began to suspect his mother wasn't the only person he'd engaged to keep her from leaving. Whether or not they believed she was his girlfriend, they definitely assumed he was in dire need of one.

She didn't figure out until after the number of guests seriously dwindled, however, that the barbecue she'd agreed to attend was for the Endeavour's immediate family members only. Even so, after the neighbors were gone, that still left quite a crowd. Dan appeared to be related to the entire population of Grand. Dallas's parents and brothers had driven the eight hours from Sweetheart and were spending the weekend in two of the bunkhouses doing double-duty as guesthouses. Ryan hadn't yet reappeared, but if anyone currently in attendance belonged to him, they weren't admitting to it.

They'd hired a caterer to serve up roast pig, which had been turning on a spit over a slow open fire since the evening before. Three chefs manned barbecues cooking steak, hamburgers, and hotdogs for the kids. One white-clothed table supported an assortment of side salads and great pots of chili. Another was weighted down with desserts. Floodlights skirted a football field disguised as a yard between the house, the garage, and the bunkhouses. They blinked on, bright enough to blind anyone not quick enough to look away. Someone had hooked up a sound system and Little Big Town crooned beneath a full moon boldly nudging stars out of its path as it trekked the night sky.

Jazz found a stray bale of hay to use as a bench, dragged

it out of the light glaring down on the tables of food, and settled a heaping plateful of roast pork and potato salad on her lap. The hay scratched at the backs of her bare legs, but not uncomfortably so. She'd had a fun day, but the attention had fast become overwhelming.

Dan popped up out of nowhere to set two plastic cups full of beer next to her feet, then returned a few moments later with a plate of food of his own. He swung a leg over the bale to drop down beside her. The baler twine holding the flakes of hay together strained under their combined weight. Her breathing became a whole lot less sure of itself. Meanwhile, as the length of his thigh pressed tight against hers, her senses grew sharper.

He had to be the luckiest human being on the face of the earth. He was tall, blond, and owned a perpetual smile that made him that much more gorgeous. He had family and friends who loved him to the point she might be a little jealous. He had a great job and he'd lucked into money. To top it all off, he was turning out to be every bit as nice as he seemed. Life wasn't fair.

"For people who got so much enjoyment out of watching you botch an interview, they've expended a great deal of effort in selling your best features to me," she said, making a superhuman effort of her own to ignore how close they sat to each other. She cut off a small piece of meat and popped it into her mouth. The smoky morsel fell apart on her tongue and she savored the taste before swallowing. The caterer really knew what he was doing. "My favorite was your grandfather. He told me not to listen to all the wild stories about you. He says it's normal for 'a young fella to try out the local talent,' as he put it."

"Granddad's in his nineties and getting senile," Dan said. "If you listen to all the wild stories about him when he was young, you'd understand why he thinks that's normal. He didn't try to put his hand up your skirt, did he?"

"Of course not," Jazz lied. His grandfather had lost his filter but was otherwise harmless. She lifted one of the plastic cups and took a careful sip of the beer. It was frothy and cold, and not at all what she expected. She examined the cup. "What am I drinking?"

"There's a new brew master in Grand. We ordered a few different kegs from her brewery for the weekend. We're drinking the lobster—the brochure claims it's a recipe from the east coast of Canada. I probably should have asked if you're allergic to shellfish." A hint of concern pinched his eyebrows together. "You aren't, are you?"

The beer was salty and hoppy, and somewhat tangy, and if Dan hadn't said anything, she might not have pinpointed the faint taste of crustacean. It really was good. "No."

"Good to hear. I'd hate to put you in the hospital on our first date."

She wondered when he was going to get tired of that joke.

It did feel like a date, though.

The evening wore on. The younger children fell asleep on the grass and were carried off to bed. She finished her meal and the beer. The air had lost the sun's direct heat, but the night remained warm.

"I should get back to the base," she finally said.

"Afraid that's not possible just yet." He locked his fingers together and stretched his arms over his head, slanting a sidelong look at her while pretending to study the sky. "You can't drive—you've been drinking. You'll have to stick around a while longer."

Jazz peered into her empty cup. She'd sipped at it for the better part of the evening, so his objection didn't carry a whole lot of weight.

"You gave me the beer. Isn't this considered entrapment?" she asked.

"You could always file a complaint with the local sheriff and find out. While you're waiting for his legal opinion," he said, hauling her to her feet, "you won't want to miss the trail ride I have planned. What do you say?"

Chapter Eight

THE BEER HAD to be doing its job because she said yes.

He wasn't about to give her a chance to change her mind, either. He'd watched her all afternoon, worried she might leave before he had a change to be alone with her again, and he wasn't waiting one minute longer.

Solar torches cast a warm yellow glow across the path as they walked behind the bunkhouses to the stables. The light above the wide double doors revealed an empty barnyard.

"Where is everyone?" Jazz asked.

"There was limited seating. Lucky for you, I know the owner and scored us two spots."

He saddled the horses. He'd picked a sweet little palomino mare for Jazz. His gelding was a sorrel with a little more spunk. Since Jazz wasn't an experienced rider, he didn't allow her to help. Neither of them needed to be riding their horse upside down in the dark if a saddle tipped sideways.

They set out along a tractor road that divided the fields. A full moon lit their way. Back in the 1800s there'd been another ranch here, and husks of the old buildings remained to this day, but it had been bankrupted by drought and it wasn't until the land passed to the Endeavour that cattle had been reintroduced. Now, hundreds of beef—dark, restless mounds against the backdrop of night sky that touched the horizon—roamed the range. The stamp of a hoof, and the rustle of low-hanging bellies dragging through grass, combined with the voices and music ringing out from the new homestead gradually fading behind them.

The silvery waters of the Tongue River snaked to their right. They left the tractor road to pick their way through the sagebrush. Dan heard a familiar swish, then a low cooing noise, followed by two booming pops. A shadow burst out from beneath one of the shrubs. Dan's horse shied a few steps before quickly settling, but Jazz's little mare remained unperturbed.

"Greater sage-grouse," Dan said, in case she was wondering, but it turned out she wasn't.

"I thought so." She patted the palomino's neck, rewarding her for her steadfastness, and offered a few soft, complimentary words. "I've flushed them by accident before. Protecting their habitat is part of our fire management strategy."

Of course. Conservation was another one of their mandates.

A path to the water's edge cut through the trees. A stand of cottonwood stretched the length of the bank, all the way to the bend in the river, and beyond. The river widened and the current slowed at this spot. He used to come here a lot as a kid, although he'd had to sneak in from the road on the far side. Jazz wasn't the first girl he'd brought here, but he didn't intend to broadcast that fact.

He helped her dismount, then wrapped the horses' reins around the low branch of a tree. Since neither animal was skittish, he left them to graze.

"Care to join me for a swim?" he asked.

"Since I don't have a suit with me, and I really doubt if you're wearing one under your jeans, I see where this is going," she said. "I haven't been skinny-dipping since I was twelve."

Dan was curious as to who a twelve-year-old girl might go skinny-dipping with. Hopefully it was other twelve-year-old girls, although he wouldn't put money on it.

"Then you're long overdue." He started to strip. He tossed his T-shirt onto the grassy bank. His jeans quickly followed.

A fallen tree had washed up onshore, probably during the floods back in March. She took a seat and settled in, planting her elbows on her knees and her chin on her cupped hands.

"Exactly how easy do you think I am, anyway?" she asked, the same way she might quiz him on what he thought of the weather.

He paused with his thumbs hooked in the waistband of his jockeys. While it didn't sound like a serious question, he was taking no chances. "Sweetheart, you proved you aren't easy your very first day, when you told me you couldn't have dinner with me because you'd already made other plans. And then you kept turning me down every time I asked you out after that."

"Why does it always have to be dinner? Did you go to bed hungry a lot as a kid?"

"Never." He wondered if she could say the same thing, but asking was out of the question. "What can I say? I like to watch women eat."

"As far as fetishes go, that seems harmless enough," she said, proving yet again that she had a good sense of humor.

Since she hadn't raised any objections, or taken her eyes of him either, he shimmied out of his drawers and tossed them aside. Nakedness didn't bother him in the least and he was happy enough to give her a show. His body might not be up to a smokejumper's standards, but there were only so many hours in a day and it was better than most.

The waterhole wasn't deep and the current was slow. He waded in up to his waist, then made a shallow dive. He came up shaking his head and wiping his eyes. A raspy night-heron barked its indignation at the invasion before flouncing off in a huff.

"The water's fantastic," he said. "No pressure. Just making an observation."

She still hadn't moved from her perch on the log. "If I get in the water with you, what's going to happen?"

The question was almost insulting. He might have checked out more than his fair share of the local talent—

thanks, Grandad, for sharing that bit of intel—but the talent had always been willing. "Not a thing you don't want."

"What if I think I want it to happen now, but end up regretting it in the morning?"

"I can't help you out there," Dan said. "You're the one who has to live with your choices, not me."

"Fair enough. Should we have a talk about our sexual histories before we proceed?" she suggested.

He fought to keep the smile off his face. He should have known she'd do her safety checks first. "We're getting pretty clinical, but yes, maybe we should get that out of the way, since the condoms are in my jeans pocket right now."

She glanced at his jeans, then at him. "You didn't think this through, did you, Sheriff?"

He waggled his brows. "You could always bring one with you."

"Or, we could start with that talk and determine if there's a need." She launched right in. "I haven't had sex in almost a year. I'm on the pill, mostly because I work with men and you just never know, and at my last checkup I was given a clean bill of health."

He wasn't sure what she meant by, '*I work with men and you just never know,*' since it could go a few different ways, but he didn't like the sounds of it at all.

"I haven't had sex in over a year"—he pushed aside the main reason why not—"and that's definitely because I work mostly with men. I'm healthy, I use condoms because they haven't made a pill for men yet, at least not that I'm aware of, and also for protection from STDs, so I guess as long as we're willing to trust each other, this means we're both good to go."

"And thus ends the romantic prelude," she said lightly.

"Is that what you're looking for?" he asked. "Romance?" If so, she could have fooled him. He'd tried that with the invitations to dinner and she kept shooting him down. The blatant approach was garnering him much better results.

"God, no."

She caught the sides of her dress and peeled it off, over her head, and he'd have to think about how fast she'd answered him later, because she wasn't wearing a bra and her breasts were fantastic. And as for the panties?

She might as well have left them home, too.

The dress fluttered to the ground by her feet. Sadly, the panties stayed put. Well, he could work around that limitation.

She edged her way down the slight embankment to the water's edge, one arm supporting her breasts while she used the other for balance, and dipped her toes in the water.

She jerked her foot back. "That's what you call fantastic?"

Drenched in moonlight, her toned, naked body surpassed that descriptor by far. He pried his tongue free from the roof of his mouth. "If the river's too low or too warm, it carries bacteria. So yes. Once you're wet, it's just like a bathtub."

He floated on his back, letting the river's slow-swirling eddy twist him about. The river burbled over the rocks in the shallows. A fish jumped upstream. He heard the splash as its tail slapped the water. The cold wasn't affecting his interest in her in the least, so if she was playing for time, he could be patient.

She waded in until she was a few feet from where he was, then sucked in a deep breath and submerged her whole body. She came up gasping and flipped the wet, jagged bangs from her forehead.

"Still not feeling the bathwater," she spluttered.

"Give it a minute."

He had his feet under him now. The water was chest deep where he stood. He dove down, intending to grab one of her legs and drag her under again, but she moved, and the water was murky because it was night, so he couldn't see.

When he came up for air, she was ten feet away.

"Like I couldn't see that coming," she said, the eyeroll implied, and he laughed. He took a few short strokes and glided toward her, stopping a few inches away so that they almost touched. He reached out and did just that, tracking the tip of his finger down the line of her cheek, then her throat, to her bare shoulder. Her wet skin was cool but not cold, so her shiver likely had little to do with the temperature of the water. At least, that was what he hoped.

Anticipation shuddered the length of his spine. "Ready

to call this a date yet?" he asked softly.

Her upturned eyes, large and unreadable in the muted light, searched his face. "That depends. Who's Andy?"

The question brought him up short. Surprisingly, the pain and anger usually brought on by hearing Andy's name spoken out loud didn't come. At some point over the past months, it had been replaced by sadness—for who she had been, for what she could have become, and what she'd never be.

Only his mother or one of his sisters could be responsible for Jazz knowing that name, however. No doubt they thought they were doing him a favor—helping get him back in the saddle, so to speak—but she'd picked a fine time to ask.

"A girl I grew up with."

He hoped a short answer would put an end to the questions. He wasn't naturally inclined to talk about his feelings for one woman while he was naked with another.

And yet, the questions kept coming.

"Did you love her?" Jazz asked.

He went with the truth. "I did."

"Do you still love her?"

His stomach unclenched. She knew nothing of Andy or she wouldn't have asked it in those particular words, or with that faint, accusing tone. She was fishing to see if he might be cheating on someone. Thanks again went to his family for her sudden need to clarify his relationship status.

He wasn't a player. He'd never lied to a woman just to get her into bed, and he believed in dating only one woman at a time. Admittedly, though, when things began to get serious, he did have a tendency to cut and run.

Maybe that was why he found Jazz so appealing. Her work was far more interesting to her than he was.

"No." He surprised even himself with that answer. "What about you? Have you ever been in love?"

She skimmed one arm over the water, not looking at him. "From what I've seen, it's overrated."

Which wasn't an answer. Had she ever been in love?

Was she still?

The hot spurt of jealousy was rich, considering his own precarious position right now. "Exactly what have you seen of it that's left such a dazzling impression?"

"Desperation, mostly." She ducked her head under again, then bobbed to the surface, treading water. Sparkling droplets of starlight clung to her long lashes before she blinked them away.

Dan should let it go. But she'd pried into his personal life, and besides, when it came to women, he'd never been smart. He floated on his back, kicking his feet to frustrate the current, and spoke to the stars as if her answer was of no importance to him whatsoever. "Let me guess. Your showgirl mother with the fascination for cowboys likes to love them and leave them?"

"Something like that."

The carelessness of her reply said he'd gotten it wrong. So, if the showgirl mother didn't love them and leave them, then chances were good that they loved her and left her, instead. He combined that assumption with Jazz's distaste for money—or at least, for men who possessed it—and along with all of the other bits and pieces he'd gathered, he thought he had her pretty much figured out. It was so tempting to run a background check on her, just to see if the conclusions he'd drawn were accurate at all, but that would be cheating. He wanted her to tell him about herself on her own.

But that could come later. Tonight, he had other, more intimate, things he intended to learn about her.

Specifically, he wanted to know how she liked to be touched.

✳

JAZZ WATCHED DAN float beside her, idly kicking his feet.

He had a beautiful body. Long, well-formed, and muscled in an active, working man way, not through hours spent at a gym.

Even though he claimed he was no longer in love with the mysterious Andy, it was plain that they had unfinished business between them. While it was mildly unsettling to think he was here with her when he'd rather be with someone else, there was also a degree of freedom in it. No promises would need to be made. There'd be no unrealistic expectations to meet. She wouldn't be human if she didn't feel envy, but decided it didn't matter.

Besides, she didn't believe in love. Not the kind that supposedly lasted forever, at any rate. Her mother's heart had been broken—and miraculously repaired—too many times for Jazz to buy into that crock. She'd had a few flings of her own—mostly with other firefighters, although there'd been one professional bull rider because she was her mother's daughter, after all—yet not once had she been tempted to take it beyond sex.

Sex with Dan would be no different.

Now that she'd made her decision, however, she was growing increasingly impatient for him to touch her again. His hands felt like fire on her skin—and fire was something she liked very much. She reached down and shimmied out of her panties, then pitched them onto the riverbank. They caught on a fallen branch where they swayed like a white, lacy flag of surrender.

"I'm ready to call this a date," she said. "If that's the word we're using for this. There's just one more thing."

"Why am I not surprised?" Dan said to the stars. "Okay, hit me. What is it?"

"Is this a one-off, or are you looking to repeat it?"

"That depends on how good it is for both of us, don't you think?"

"Agreed. But as long as we're having sex, we only sleep

with each other. If we want other partners, we tell each other first."

"This has got to be the most clinical sexual encounter—excuse me, date—I've ever experienced... Let me guess. It's a safety issue." Humor rolled across the water's surface toward her.

"It definitely is." He was making fun of her, but she didn't care. She trusted him, but only up to a point. If Andy suddenly came back to town, she wanted to know.

"I'm good with that," he said.

He flipped to his stomach and surged to a stand. Water streamed from his hair and he wiped it away from his face. Moonlight turned his tanned upper torso to dark gold. He waded the short distance between them, reaching for her, bringing her close. Hands stroked her bare shoulders and glided up and down her arms, trailing flames. The sensations he stirred with the lightest of touches were wildly, frenetically, sexy. He nuzzled her throat and pure, greedy lust scattered her thoughts. Flames shot up the insides of her thighs.

"You are so beautiful..." he whispered. "Tell me what you like. Do you like it when I do this?" He slid one hand over her breast, gently toying with the nipple.

She palmed his buttocks and brought her belly to his, capturing the full, hard length of his erection between them. She lifted her face, inviting one of his kisses. "I do. Very much."

"How about this?" He replaced his hand with his mouth and his tongue, sucking and teasing.

She panted a little at the slow glide of his tongue and the light nip of his teeth, rising on her toes and arching her back to grant him better access as water swirled around them. She clutched at his hips to keep the insistent tug of the current from prying them apart. "A definite yes."

"This is where things can get tricky. But in case you're at all worried, I've never drowned a woman during sex before. I don't plan on you being the first."

That made her laugh. "Maybe I'll take the top position. Just to be safe."

"I have a better idea." He scooped her up, positioning her legs around his hips, and braced his back against the current so he could lean against it with his knees slightly bent. He supported her upper body with his elbows and the flats of his palms. "You're going to have to help me fit the pieces together if we want this to work."

"You mean like this?" She slid one hand between their slick bodies and found his erection, taking a moment to explore its magnificence with the tips of her fingers.

"God, that feels good." He groaned, closing his eyes as she stroked him. His breath came in short pants. He made a growling sound, more like a purr, deep in his throat, to signal his pleasure.

That half growl, combined with the way his fingers bit into the undersides of her thighs as he held her, left Jazz more than ready for him. She guided his erection into position, then slowly, carefully, eased it inside her, letting out a soft, eager cry of her own as it filled her. She didn't, however, close her eyes. The night was dark, but not so dark that she couldn't read the enjoyment playing out on Dan's face. She liked that he wasn't afraid to show how he felt. It made sex with him that much more exciting.

Carefully, so as not to tip them both into the river as water lapped at her hips, she set a rhythm. Taking things slow was a new experience for her, and she found she liked it, too. She kept one hand where their bodies joined, cradling the soft sac containing his boys in her palm, and her other arm crooked around his neck. Anticipation built in her belly. Tight inner muscles began to convulse. She clenched him hard with her legs and the arm strangling his neck. Her free hand skimmed to his buttocks, pulling him deeper inside her, trying to make it as good for him as it was for her.

Pressure mounted until she couldn't hold back any longer. Low, eager groans and words of encouragement said he, too, was close. She gasped as the sky spun out of control and stars cascaded around them. He stiffened. His fingers dug into her thighs. He let out that half growl, half purr as he came, and she slumped against him, too dazed to move.

The stars blinked and it occurred to her that this could hardly be comfortable for him. She tried to free her legs from his grasp so she could stand. He pretended to stagger, and her arms flailed to the sides, splashing water.

"Kidding. I've got you," he said, before lowering her to her feet.

They stood waist deep in the water together, limbs tangled up in each other, catching their breaths. Jazz felt the rapid drumbeat of his heart under her cheek. A light gust of wind rustled the cottonwood leaves.

His fingers tickled the length of her spine. "I'd say you did most of the work, except all of that muscle makes you pretty heavy," he said. "Not that I'm complaining, mind you. But you have no idea how hard it was to keep us both from floating away."

"Your personal sacrifice is duly noted, Sheriff. You're a real team player. But I'm getting cold."

Finding their clothes in the dark was another adventure. The light wind had lifted her panties from the branch where they'd snagged. Dan spotted a pale shadow under a bush. He scooped them up, triumphant.

"This is the best treasure hunt ever," he announced, then stuffed them into his pocket.

Jazz held up his wallet. "You're right. I found this on the ground. I don't suppose you'd consider a trade?"

"You mean these for a driver's license, a credit card, and a few condoms it turns out I don't need? I don't think so," he said.

He finally agreed to the exchange only after she pointed out that sitting in a saddle was going to prove exceedingly uncomfortable without panties.

"But you owe me," he said.

They began the ride back to the ranch. A blaze of light against the night sky marked its location. The rumble of music meant the blind could find it easily, too. She darted sideways glances at Dan.

She'd been wrong. Sex with him was nothing like anything she'd had before. It was intimate, and fun, and required a decent amount of skill with calisthenics. Communication skills were another requirement, because without them, someone would drown. Definitely not a one-off, at least as far as she was concerned.

But it was still sex.

Chapter Nine

T HEY RODE SIDE by side in the moonlight, the horses picking their own path and taking their time.

Dan was in no hurry either. When they got to the ranch they'd be back among people and he liked having Jazz all to himself. The downside to the open house he'd planned with her in mind was that somehow, it had morphed into a family weekend retreat.

Each of the ranch house's three separate wings had six bedrooms—he had no idea why, since they were all single men, but Ryan had insisted—and Dan's parents, his sisters and their husbands, and the youngest nieces and nephews had commandeered all five of the spare rooms in his. Dallie and Ryan's homes had been similarly invaded. While Ryan had no family he laid claim to, not since his mother passed away a few years ago, he loved hanging out with Dan and Dallie's. The bunkhouses were full of teenagers and young adults. No danger in that.

He could hardly suggest Jazz spend the remainder of the night with him when the two sets of twin terrors rose at the crack of dawn and knew where he slept. As much as he loved his nieces and nephews, he knew whose face he'd rather wake up to.

She helped him unsaddle the horses, then bed them down for the night. Once that was finished, they started up the path to the house. Someone had a guitar out and people were singing. It was mostly off-key and the accuracy of the lyrics could be called into question. No one in this crew was going to make it on *America's Got Talent*.

These were the people he loved most in the world and he liked how well Jazz had fit in with them earlier.

She veered off toward the garage, where she'd parked her bike.

"Aren't you coming back to the party?" he asked.

She tucked the short skirt of her dress between her thighs and swung one leg over the seat of the bike. "It's got to be well after midnight. The guys will think I'm dead in a ditch."

He eyed the bike. They'd have good reason to think that. "Let me get my keys and I'll drive you home."

She smiled up at him as she raised the kickstand with her foot. "I feel like we've had this conversation before." With a flick of her thumb and her wrist, the engine rumbled to life.

He hooked his thumbs in the waist of his jeans and watched her ride off. She had no jacket. No helmet, either. And there was no law against it.

He sighed. He hadn't even gotten a kiss good night. He hoped she didn't assume this was a one-off, because if so, she was sadly mistaken.

On the one hand, it was a significant benefit to the Endeavour that she was so committed to her career. The base gave him no worries at all while she was in charge. She knew what she was doing and had everything under control.

On the other hand, however...

Her aversion to commitment put any issues he might have on that same subject to shame. Chasing after women who didn't want to be caught didn't exactly catapult him into the genius arena, either. The trouble was, now that he'd had a sample of what Jazz had to offer, he hungered for more.

He never learned.

He had no urge to face a family inquisition just yet on a subject he didn't understand either, so he veered into the garage for a few quiet moments. He groped for the switch on the wall and the room flooded with light. It took a moment for his eyes to adjust, but when they did, he and Ryan—who was seated at the wheel of a really sweet, steel-blue AMG S65 sedan—blinked at each other.

Dan did a mental double take. Ryan had some odd personal quirks, but this was weird, even for him. What was he doing sitting in a car in the garage at one in the morning with all the lights out?

"Hey, Bruce Wayne. Got anything you'd like to talk about?"

"Not really," Ryan said.

Dan shut off the overhead light. The luminous moon

glowed through the roof panels, bright enough for him to navigate his way to the car. He popped the passenger door open, crammed his considerable body inside, and sank into the embrace of the softest leather his butt had ever encountered. There was a lot to be said for riding in comfort—he got that, because as a county sheriff, he spent a lot of time in his car—but this was extreme.

"Where've you been hiding all day?" he asked.

"I took a drive to Greybull."

"Greybull… as in Wyoming?" That was four hours away. An eight-hour round trip.

Ryan nodded.

Dan scrubbed his eyebrow with his thumb. "Why?"

"Why not?"

"Sure you don't have anything you'd like to talk about?"

"I'm sure."

Dan was at a loss. Ryan's grand theft auto career had begun when he was twelve or thirteen. Counselors claimed cars represented freedom to him, and he'd never outgrown the obsession. While these days he bought his own rather than resorting to theft, an eight-hour road trip out of state meant something big weighed on his mind. It might or might not have anything to do with the Endeavour and the money. Managing both was an enormous undertaking, but Ryan had shown no signs of it being too much for him. If anything, it gave him purpose.

Worry wriggled around in Dan's gut. He didn't give a

damn about the money, although he'd admit he was fond of the ranch. He did care where the money came from, however. But Ryan had sworn it was legitimate and Dan believed him.

"How did the open house go?" Ryan asked.

"Pretty much perfect."

"I take it by your big, goofy smile that you finally made headway with Jazz?"

"I don't know what you're talking about."

"I heard her bike leaving just now."

Dan changed the subject. "You missed the barbecue. Our moms were asking about you."

Ryan had boarded with the Tuckers when he worked as a dude wrangler at the Bar-No Sweetheart Ranch in Sweetheart for a few summers. Now that he and Dallas both lived in Grand, Dan's mother treated them like her own. Ryan loved the attention.

"I'll be around for the rest of the weekend, so I'll see them tomorrow. Are they cooking breakfast, by any chance?" His eyes lit with hope.

"They were planning to set up a breakfast buffet in the common room, so it seems you're in luck."

Ryan was about to comment when the side door opening and closing interrupted whatever he had to say. Overhead lights blazed. Dan and Ryan turned their heads.

Dallas stared back.

He wore a navy-colored med school grad T-shirt that

had seen better days, baggy beige cargo shorts, and flip-flops. Black, shaggy curls looked even more disheveled than normal. He looked like he should be backpacking around South America and camping on beaches rather than manning a free medical clinic in rural Montana. And yet looks could be deceiving. When Dallas set a goal for himself, he let nothing stand in his way.

He was a lot like Ryan in that regard. The difference between them, however, was that Dallas had always wanted to be a doctor whereas Ryan didn't yet know what he wanted to be when he grew up—other than a cowboy, of course.

"Well, if this is where the new weekly briefings are being held…" The room plunged back into shadow. Seconds later, the rear passenger door opened and then Dallas was hanging over the backs of their seats, his face in between them. "I'm not sure why we have to conduct them in the dark, but okay."

"I'm not sure why we bothered building the common area," Dan replied. He half-turned so he could see Dallas better. The leather creaked. "Ryan's cars are more comfortable, and as an added bonus, they're mobile."

"You can take the man out of the mobile, but you can't take the mobile out of the man," Dallas agreed, nodding.

"What does that even mean?" Ryan asked.

Dallas shrugged. "You missed the excitement. Dan gave an interview to *Entertainment News Nightly* and it got picked up by national news stations."

Dan turned to stare. "It did not."

"Indeed it did, my friend. Just a few seconds worth of coverage, mind you—enough for the entire country to learn that sadly, our hottest new sheriff billionaire is already off the market. Snatched up by some local Daisy Mae. Maybe not in those exact words."

Dan really, really hoped not. He doubted very much if Jazz would find it funny.

"Who's Daisy Mae?" Ryan asked.

"An anatomically incorrect cartoon character who dresses in skimpy shorts that are going to cause her any number of health issues. Married to Li'l Abner?"

Ryan shot Dallas a withering glance. "I meant, who's the local Daisy Mae?"

"Oh. That would be Jazz."

"Get out of town." Ryan's head swiveled toward Dan. "I was only kidding about you making headway with her. I didn't get the impression she's all that into you."

She was into him, all right. He tried not to think of the soft little sounds she'd made in his ear while she proved it. He'd savor that memory later.

"What's so hard to believe? Maybe she succumbed to my many charms."

His so-called friends burst out laughing.

"Dan was about to get his ass handed to him by a reporter so I asked Jazz to help bail him out," Dallas explained. "When the reporter asked her who she was, the opportunist here"—he gestured at Dan—"jumped in and claimed she was his girlfriend. Then he milked it for the rest of the day." He flicked Dan's shoulder with the back of his hand. "You owe me for that, by the way."

If memory served him, Dallas had left him to fend for himself and it was only good luck that Jazz happened along. He was in too good a mood to challenge him on it however, especially since things had worked out for the best as far as he was concerned.

"I'll write you a check."

"Seriously, Dan. Are you really interested in her?" Ryan asked.

Dan sincerely hoped Ryan wasn't interested in Jazz, too. He might be one of his best friends, but he was also too late. "What if I am?"

"Quit looking at me like that. She's not my type." Ryan's eyes held a hint of worry—something else Dan didn't like, because it meant there was a *but* coming. "I like her. Don't get me wrong," Ryan continued. "But"—and there it was—"she's very focused on her career. She likes a challenge. There's not a huge demand in the marketplace for smoke-jumpers or base managers, so her options are limited in terms of opportunities for advancement. I'm pretty sure our piddly little Custer County base isn't going to satisfy her for longer than it takes her to find something better."

Dan read between the lines and got what Ryan didn't want to come right out and say—she wasn't going to be satisfied with the local sheriff either, no matter how rich he was. In fact, Jazz being Jazz, the money didn't really even work in his favor.

"I disagree." Dallas stuck his oar in the water. "Fire-fighting communities are pretty tight-knit. Now that Jazz isn't a smokejumper anymore, she's looking for a place to belong. A home. You could always offer her a permanent position at the base and see what happens," he suggested. "There are lots of things she could do around here during the off season."

"That's a terrible idea. What if it doesn't work out? What's Dan supposed to do then? Fire her?" Ryan, the voice of doom, demanded.

Dan decided it was time to put the brakes on this conversation. They'd talked about women plenty of times in the past, but he didn't want to discuss Jazz and where she might see herself in a few years. "You're getting ahead of yourselves. We haven't even discussed who gets custody of the kids yet."

"You've got to be kidding." Dallas shifted his weight in the back seat, which put the car's rear suspension system to the test. "She actually slept with you?"

Dan sifted through what he'd just said and couldn't come up with a thing that would cause him to reach that conclusion. There was no figuring out what went on in the guy's head. "Whatever gave you that idea?"

"In order to have kids, you have to have sex. Did no one ever explain basic biology to you?"

Dan decided to neither confirm nor deny. "I know this will come as a shock, but there are parts of my life that are none of your business. This is one of those parts."

Dallas nodded his understanding. "That's probably wise. I can't keep a secret."

"You're a doctor," Ryan said to him. "Aren't you supposed to swear to respect the privacy of your patients?"

"Which is why you didn't hear from me about the giant boil on Weldon Scott's nethers that I lanced," Dallas replied. "I've never seen anything like it. Except on YouTube maybe. Besides, you guys aren't my patients."

While Dan highly doubted that Weldon had a boil on his nether regions—or any of his regions, for that matter—this seemed like a good opportunity to call it a night.

He opened the car door. "I'll see you guys in the morning."

He was in bed with the lights out before it occurred to him that, while Weldon Scott's boil might have deflected the topic of conversation off him and Jazz, and Ryan had managed to divert Dan's attention away from whatever darkness plagued him, neither one of them knew what Dallas had been doing in the garage so late at night, too.

✴

JAZZ WAS MONITORING a wildfire in Southern California when her cell phone pealed out "Dancing Queen" and broke her concentration.

She flipped off the ringer, although the phone continued to vibrate on her desk. Eli, sitting beside her, asked her a question she didn't quite catch. She removed one of her earbuds and he asked it again.

"Aren't you going to get that?"

"No."

There could be only a few reasons why her mother would call, none of them good, and they all involved money. She had far more important things to worry about at the moment.

It looked as if she'd have to deploy smokejumpers to California and she was both nervous and jealous—nervous because she had other people's lives to consider, and there was nothing she could do to help them if anything should go wrong, and jealous because she desperately wished she could go with them. Sitting in an office all day made her restless. She missed the outdoors.

The icon on her phone signaling she'd received a voicemail lit up. She planned on ignoring that, too. She settled her earbud back in place.

Eli, however, was ready to take a break from whatever work he was only half doing.

"When are you going to tell everyone that you and the big boss are an item, Tinkerbell?" he asked, louder this time so she couldn't miss it. "We've been waiting for the official announcement."

She looked up from her monitor and removed her earbud. Again. Maybe she hadn't heard him correctly. "What was that?"

He took a sip of his morning coffee. Innocent eyes regarded her over the rim of his mug. The corners of his mouth twitched. "You and Dan were on the news the other night. I must say, you make a good-looking couple."

She couldn't believe the local news had picked up such a ridiculous story, but then again, Dan was the sheriff, which made him a public figure in Custer County. He didn't get to put "reclusive billionaire" on his CV.

And to be fair, she'd known better than to get involved with her boss. Besides, she hadn't heard from him in almost a week—although that in itself likely meant nothing. He was a busy man. There was no need to be miffed that he hadn't so much as texted.

"We're not a couple," she said.

"Didn't your mother ever talk to you about not giving the milk away for free?" Eli persisted.

As the only woman on base, she was used to the guys' teasing. But the next few weeks were going to be excruciating. She didn't have a prayer that the gossip hadn't spread through the entire team by now.

"Very funny." Her face had turned red, which gave away a lot more than milk. "One of his partners asked me to pass him an urgent message and the reporter chose to interpret it the wrong way," she felt compelled to explain, although it sounded lame, even to her, meaning she was only making things worse.

Eli couldn't hold back his grin any longer. "I get it. There have got to be dozens of ways to interpret him telling the world you're his girlfriend."

"He was joking. Do you mind? I'm busy." She wiggled the earbud into place and returned to her screen.

Her attention, however, was now only half on her work.

She'd had a good time with Dan and his family. Especially with Dan. More importantly, she liked him. A lot. He was good-natured and smart and incredibly capable in any number of ways. There didn't seem to be much that he couldn't handle.

But while those qualities were attractive, therein lay the danger. It would be too easy to sit around and wait for him to call, then be crushed when he didn't.

Fortunately, she'd learned a lot from observing her mother, who'd proven incapable of recognizing that the men she slept with were operating catch and release programs, and she'd taken into consideration the possibility this might happen with Dan. It had nothing to do with whether or not he was a player, and everything to do with Andy, the girl who still had a priority position in his heart. She simply wasn't so foolish as to become attached to a man who had a history of keeping his options open where another woman was concerned.

Since he'd done the pursuing up to this point, she saw no

value in changing the rules. He'd call her when he had time. If he didn't call, she'd simply suffer it out until October and chalk it up to another life lesson confirmed.

Chapter Ten

S HE DEPLOYED HER three-man team a little after one
o'clock in the afternoon.

Envy returned in full force as she helped with the
equipment checks in the ready room. Each of the packs
weighed in at one hundred and twenty pounds. Hers had
been no exception when she was jumping, and she'd taken a
lot of pride in it.

Within ten minutes the men had suited up, climbed into
their plane, and were gone. She watched the plane taxi down
the runway, soar into the sky, then vanish from sight.

At least I'm still part of the team.

Although, right now, as she stood on the tarmac watching others fly off to adventure, that was small consolation.
She might be part of the team, but she was no longer part of
that tight inner circle. She was barely thirty years old. Was
this really where she saw herself for the next thirty-five or
more years? Watching others do what she'd done and taken
such pride in? Work that she'd loved?

The worry was something she hadn't considered when
she'd taken the management position. She'd drafted the

operations plan that was supposed to keep the team safe. What if unanticipated conditions arose and they changed it? What if they didn't? What if she'd made a mistake and it cost them their lives?

She had a few hours to kill while the team was in flight and she could use a distraction. Not to mention a haircut. Now might be a good time to check out one of the hair salons in Grand.

A half hour later, she parked her bike on Yellowstone Drive.

The temperature had soared into the upper nineties and was fast approaching one hundred degrees. Low, angry gray clouds in the distance threatened rain and the humidity was high. She peeled off the one-piece mesh suit she used for biking on hot days and exchanged boots for her flip-flops, then stowed all her gear. Underneath the suit, she wore a pale blue tank top and white shorts. She set off on foot, her flip-flops slapping her heels and her shoulder bag banging her hip, to find the salon where she'd called ahead for an appointment.

Yellowstone Drive meandered alongside the Yellowstone River. A number of one and two-story businesses with a wide boardwalk behind them snaked the river side of the street. The sheriff's office squatted between the Custer County courthouse and a law firm. The sign outside of the law firm proudly proclaimed it *Grand Cooper and Nash*. A small café a few doors down from the law firm boasted an outdoor deck that extended past the boardwalk and over the lazy river. It smelled delicious as Jazz walked past. She'd have to stop for a latte on her way back to the base. Lou's Pub was buried between the bank and the Grand Hotel, the lone three-story building on the street.

People on the street all seemed to know her, which still took getting used to, but their familiarity was growing on her. Quite a few waved in a friendly, absentminded manner, the way they'd acknowledge a neighbor they liked even though they had nothing in common.

She found the salon across the street from the hotel and pushed through shiny glass doors right on time. A welcome blast of cool air hit her, along with the smells of hair coloring and spray. The woman at reception had a round, pleasant face, warm brown eyes, and short brown hair highlighted with platinum-blond streaks to within an inch of its life.

The warmth spread from her eyes to her cheeks. "You must be our two o'clock, Jazz. Come with me."

She bustled around the counter and led Jazz through the open door to a room with three chairs facing brightly lit mirrors. Jazz was uneasy about entrusting her hair to an unknown stylist, but she had little choice. The cut had grown out and was becoming unruly.

She found herself seated next to a pretty woman about her own age. The other woman smiled at her in the mirror while the stylist blow-dried her long hair.

"Hi. You must be the new base manager everyone is talking about. I'm Lacey Anderson. I teach at Marion Street Grand Elementary. And this is Lydia."

On Lacey's far side, a gorgeous little girl with the greenest eyes Jazz had ever seen sat patiently waiting. Her fluffy, dark blond hair, already deepening to brown, had been freshly styled with a bright blue ribbon and bow. If she was Lacey's daughter then she must take after her father, because they looked nothing alike.

Jazz's stylist introduced herself as Simone. She was slender and pretty, but in a harsh, brittle way, as if life treated her rough—or vice versa. Her blond hair, scraped back in a high ponytail, came from a bottle. The dishwater roots gave it away. Fine lines pinched the corners of golden-brown eyes. A pale blue smock covered navy capris and a red T-shirt.

"First, let's get you shampooed. Then we can talk about what you want to have done," Simone said briskly.

As Jazz started to follow her to the shampoo station, the door of the shop opened and one of the finest Montana males she'd ever seen walked through it. He was tall and broad-shouldered, even bigger than Dan, with close-cut black hair and eyes of such a striking shade of green she could identify the color from across the shop. The little girl had to be his, even though except for the eyes they didn't look much alike, either. He wore dusty jeans and boots and a long-sleeved shirt despite the heat, suggesting he'd been hard at work and was taking a break.

"Jake's here," the receptionist called out from the front

desk, and Lacey's face lit up in a way that left no doubt as to her feelings about that. Lydia slid out of her chair and made a dash for the door, so her feelings on the announcement were no great secret, either.

"Excuse me, ma'am," Jake said to her, crouching down to her level. "Have you seen my little girl? Lacey was supposed to bring her here for a haircut."

Lydia's giggles were the only other thing Jazz overheard before she was settled at a sink, but the whole scene was pretty cute. Men who knew how to communicate with children pushed the buttons of every woman of child-bearing age and beyond, and even though she had no desire for any of her own, she was no exception. She wondered what their story was.

It didn't take her long to find out. The trio was leaving the shop as Jazz and her freshly washed, towel-wrapped hair were being hustled back to Simone's workstation.

"It's such a shame what happened to the McGregors," Simone said.

Her tone suggested she was open to questions, but Jazz didn't bite. Any tragedy that had befallen the McGregors was their business, not hers.

Simone didn't share her opinion, however. "Jake's parents, his sister, and his sister's husband were killed in a plane crash in Peru last year. Now Jake and his brothers are raising his sister's children."

The name McGregor was ringing a bell. "I've met a

Mara McGregor."

The comment had seemed innocent enough on the surface, but Simone had been given an opening and Jazz was soon filled in on the whole McGregor saga. Jake and Lacey were engaged to be married. Jake had custody of Lydia and her two older brothers, Mac and Finn. Mara, a famous dancer, was married to Luke, who ran the Wagging Tongue Ranch with his brother Jake. Luke was some kind of genius who also taught college-level computer courses. Mara and Luke had a baby boy. The youngest McGregor, Zack, was married to Posey, who'd moved to Grand from Boston early last spring. She had a cute little girl named Trixie, and she and Zack were expecting a new baby together any day now. Zack, a former accountant, worked on the Running River Ranch with Weldon Scott. Rumor had it that Weldon would sell the ranch to Zack when he retired and Zack would combine that operation with the one his two brothers ran.

"Zack and Dan McKillop are good friends," Simone added, leaving a long pause for any comment.

Jazz murmured "*Oh?*" in an effort to be polite. She had no desire to become the next hot topic of salon conversation—although she suspected that ship had already sailed. The other two chairs were empty and the stylists had gone off on break, leaving her alone with Simone.

And Simone, it turned out, could be persistent.

"I dated Dan for a few months. Of course, that was a long time ago, before he had money." She fussed with Jazz's hair, measuring a section with her fingers and then taking a few snips off at the crown. She kept her eyes on her task. "You've probably already heard that he's got a bit of a reputation with the women in Grand. Don't get me wrong—he's not a cheat. He gives you his full attention when he's with you, and when he's ready to move on, he's honest about it. But he gets bored easily. Enjoy it while it lasts."

Jazz couldn't decide who she was more annoyed with— Dan for an irritating joke that had grown legs or Simone for her need to issue a warning that, without a doubt, stemmed from jealousy.

Then she decided she felt sorry for Dan. Simone too, for that matter. Dan, because while he might get bored easily, in reality he hadn't yet found anyone who could measure up to Andy, the woman he'd loved. And Simone, because her need to mention Dan's money was a strong indicator that she might have tried harder to hang on to him if she'd had that as an incentive. She was the type of woman Jazz did not, under any circumstances, intend to become.

"I'm only here for the summer," she said, and inadvertently launched the conversation in a whole new direction.

Interest etched Simone's features. "I can only imagine the stories the smokejumpers must tell. What's it like to work with them? Do you all live at the base twenty-four hours a day?"

Jazz was used to answering questions about what it was

like to be the only woman working with men, and what the sleeping arrangements were. But it came as a shock to realize Simone didn't know she was a smokejumper, too.

Or rather, she used to be one.

"They're a great group of guys who are all married. They spend their off-hours FaceTiming with their families. I've known most of them for years. Their wives, too," she said.

If Simone was disappointed not to get any base gossip, she didn't let on. Instead, she began to blow-dry Jazz's hair. When she was done, she passed Jazz a small hand mirror so she could examine the back.

"It looks fantastic," Simone said proudly. "The style suits you."

Jazz tipped the mirror to check it out from several angles. It did look good. She'd worried for nothing. She couldn't have gotten a better cut from her favorite stylist in Helena.

She thanked Simone, paid at reception and left her a hefty tip, then stepped into the sweltering heat. The gray clouds had moved in and their swollen bellies appeared ready to let go any second.

The clouds split apart and their contents descended in one mighty torrent. She had no umbrella and nowhere to shelter. She ducked back under the awning, but it offered very little protection. In another thirty seconds or so, she'd be soaked.

So much for the hundred dollars she'd just spent on her hair.

The sheriff's SUV pulled up to the curb, its windshield wipers whipping frantically back and forth, unable to keep pace with the downpour. Dan leaned across the front seat and threw open the door.

"Get in."

She was ridiculously happy to see him. All of her earlier concerns about catch and release programs flew straight out of the window. She dashed from the protection of the awning and ducked through the open SUV door, slamming it closed behind her. Her bare feet slid in her wet flip-flops. Rain drummed on the roof and streamed down the glass, but inside, it was cozy and dry.

"Your hair looks great," he said.

"Thank you."

Since she'd been standing outside a salon there was no need to read too much into his observational skills. But she totally got what Simone meant about him giving a woman his full attention. The way he looked at her with those country star eyes had her heart free-falling.

It filled her with terror.

✳

DAN HAD NEVER seen a woman's expression change from pleasure to fear with such rapid speed, before. He wondered what he'd done to trigger it.

Since Jazz had come from the salon where Simone

worked, that might explain it. Simone had stopped by his office a few times over the past months, dropping hints she'd like to pick up where they'd left off.

Dan had no guilt with regard to Simone and how things had ended between them. She liked to party, and while he enjoyed a few beers with friends, he hadn't been able to keep pace with her and hold down a job, too. They'd grown bored with each other.

Jazz didn't strike him as the type of woman who'd lend too much weight to any tales a former girlfriend might tell her, though. Whatever he'd done to make her look at him that way, he'd undo. He'd had a rough week juggling budgets, both at home and at work. The jail food provision account was always a contentious election issue and he made sure every penny was accounted for. He could fill out the paperwork in his sleep. So far, catching sight of her had been the highlight of the day. She always looked so fresh and pretty. The fringe of blond hair over her eyes made them look larger and even more blue. If she ever decided to wear makeup—which she didn't need—she'd no doubt be stunning, but he much preferred her this way.

He'd learned his lesson about offering her a lift home, but she couldn't ride her bike until the downpour let up and he was due for a break. He had an errand to run in Billings, but he didn't have to make that trip today. "How about we go grab a coffee and wait for the rain to stop?"

"I'd love a coffee. I'd planned to stop at the Wayside Café on my way home."

The Wayside wasn't anywhere near private enough for his liking. "I have someplace better in mind."

He checked for traffic in his mirrors, then made an illegal U-turn in the middle of the street. Seconds later, he pulled into his parking spot outside of his office.

"Your office coffee is better than the Wayside Café's?" she asked, giving him quite the side-eye of disbelief.

"Your skepticism wounds me. But I never said the coffee was better. I said the place was."

"What's so special about your office?"

"It's empty. We can be alone."

Her eyes darkened and her tone cooled. "I'm not a booty call, Sheriff."

He rushed to reverse the impression he'd given. "Good to know. I'm not, either." Although honestly, he could be swayed because he wasn't proud. "But I've had a long week and I'd really like to enjoy your company without having to listen to a list of grievances from everyone who happens along."

Her gaze softened, and some of the earlier pleasure he'd seen in her eyes reemerged. "I can understand that. I'd like to have coffee with you, wherever you like." She made a move to open her door.

"Wait. Stay right there."

He dug around in the back for the umbrella he kept on hand for emergencies, found it jammed lengthwise under the seat, then got out of the car, opened the umbrella, and dashed around the hood to the passenger side. He popped open her door and held the umbrella for her. He anchored his free arm around her shoulders and together, they dashed to the side door of the building as sheets of rain pounded the pavement around them and bounced half a foot in the air.

The interior of the building was hardly cool. The air-conditioning in the old structure was sketchy at best and the temperature hovered around the low nineties. The air smelled of old coffee, dry books, and funky foot odor.

To their right was the reception area, currently unstaffed. The admin assistant worked Wednesdays and Thursdays and all four of the deputies were out of the office. There was a small kitchenette and an office supply cabinet straight ahead, and to the left, Dan's office and the boardroom. All of the squat, horizontally oriented windows hung slightly below the ceiling, too high off the floor and too stubby for anyone to climb through. The building had once been the jail, although the current lockup was now attached to the back of the courthouse.

He led the way to his office. It contained an old wooden desk with an oversized leather chair, a comfortable red leather visitor chair that had seen better days, a portly filing cabinet, laptop, and a small round glass meeting table flanked by two solid oak, antique spool chairs with leather seats. The last sheriff who'd sat in this office had served for forty-seven years, and except for the few pieces of art Dan had contributed, he liked it the way it had been left to him. He fervently prayed that the interior designer who'd desecrated his home never visited here. Rain bashed on the roof. The red light on his phone blinked, but he didn't bother checking his messages. If something urgent came up in the next hour, a deputy would call him on his cell.

Jazz tucked her hands into the front pockets of her tight shorts and took it all in. A tiny frown furrowed fine lines at her brow. "The *Dogs Playing Poker* painting is a nice touch."

"I got it at an auction."

He was proud of it, too. He'd always wanted a man cave and this was as close to one as he was likely to get. Having money meant others constantly had opinions as to how he should spend it, but here—pardon the pun—his word was law.

Even so, he waited to hear what she thought.

"You're such a guy."

"Thank you," he said, and she laughed up at him with her eyes and a slight curve of her mouth.

That laugh on her lips was magnetic. It pulled him to her. He eased his arms around her and lowered his head, covering her mouth with his, and at the moment of contact, lust exploded. She tasted like lip balm and mint, which he was very familiar with by now, and he drew in the scent of her freshly cut hair. Her palms nestled at the small of his back and the tip of her tongue stroked his bottom lip, and he was so hard for her, he ached.

He used to pride himself on his self-control. Not any-more.

Awareness jabbed him in the chest, knocking the breath from his lungs. Physically, he'd found her pretty hard to resist from day one, which came as no real surprise. He tended to gravitate toward the blond, athletic, independent type. But she was also smart, she was funny, and she got to him in a way few women did. He was falling for her. Hard.

Much, much, too hard, given how skittish she was when it came to relationships.

Then again, he couldn't really claim to be an expert at them. What he'd had with Andy had been completely dysfunctional and pretty one-sided. He wanted something different with Jazz. Something more mutual. And stable.

Did he know how to pick women or what?

"I'm reconsidering my stand on booty calls," Jazz said.

Dan needed no second invitation. The slight glaze to her eyes hinted that she wasn't immune to him, either. He got rid of his sidearm, then hooked a finger in the front of her shorts. He nudged them down her hips to her knees, taking the panties with them. She had her hands bunched in his shirt, working the buttons free and exposing his chest, as she kicked off her flip-flops and shorts. He yanked at the hem of her T-shirt, turning it inside out as he drew it over her head. Her breasts were even more amazing by daylight. He licked her nipples, first one, then the other, until they both stood at attention. He nipped at one rosy tip, savoring the taste as he drew it into his mouth. Her moan of pleasure caught in her throat and she arched her back, driving him mad. She unzipped his trousers and had him cupped in her warm hand within seconds, stroking him with a delicate touch as he eased his palm between her thighs. He found her warm and ready for him, and if he wasn't inside of her within the next minute or two, things would progress embarrassingly fast.

"Tell me what you want," he said. He already knew she wasn't shy.

"I want you to touch me. Like this," she commanded, guiding two of his fingers inside her. He stroked long and deep until her breath came in short pants. "Oh, my God, yes," she cried out. "Now, Dan. I need you."

He freed himself from his trousers, hiked her into his arms, and managed to get them both into his chair with her on his lap. Within seconds he was fully engulfed by the fire inside her, and she was riding him hard, her legs straddling his. He covered her breasts with his hands and closed his eyes, thrusting his hips upward to match her downward movements, letting her set the pace. He felt the start of her orgasm, the tiny vaginal muscles contracting, the pressure and intensity building until it was almost too much for him to bear. He gritted his teeth, determined that she would come first. Then she cried out his name and so much for that. He came so hard and fast lights flickered behind his eyelids.

When the world finally settled to rights, she was flopped

against him. Sweat slickened their bodies. The rain had eased up. It no longer pounded on the roof.

"Next time, I swear—we're going to try this in a bed," he said, stroking her hair. Her breath was warm on his throat. He could sit with her like this forever.

"I have no complaints," she replied.

Her phone, half-lodged in her clothing, vibrated on the floor.

She scrambled off his lap, grabbed her panties and shorts and jerked them up her thighs, and fumbled it from her pocket. "I've got to get that. My team is on its way to Southern California and I've been waiting for word."

Chapter Eleven

THE WORD WASN'T the one Jazz had been expecting.

"Why didn't you tell me you were dating a billionaire?" her mother demanded.

The question came through loud and shrill and impossible for Dan not to overhear in the quiet room, since he had his arms around her with his cheek pressed tight to hers. The scruff of hair on his chest tickled the bare skin between her shoulders.

She should know by now to check numbers first. She'd completely forgotten her mother had been trying to reach her. "I'm busy. Can I call you back?"

"No, you can't," her mother snapped. "I've been trying to reach you all week. You don't return my calls, and half the time, you don't answer. Why did I have to learn about this on the news? Do you have any idea how humiliating it is for me to have to answer questions when I haven't been given the news by my own daughter?"

There was no hope that Dan wasn't getting all this. He'd tightened his hold on her waist, not even trying to pretend he wasn't listening in. What a difference there was between his mother and hers. She considered hanging up, but there was no point in it now.

"What kind of questions are you getting?" she asked, because why not wind her mother up a bit more?

Jazz already knew what kind of questions they'd be and where they'd likely originated. Her mother often owed money to old friends from her showgirl days. She should tell her she wasn't alone, but it was too late for that. She'd never be able to look Dan in the eye again as it was.

"This is so typical of you. You don't tell me anything. I didn't even know you weren't in Helena, anymore."

"I'm never in Helena in the summers." Jazz couldn't stop herself from pointing that out. "I've been fighting wildfires around the country out of Missoula for years. Right now, I'm working as a base manager for Custer County. Hopefully next year it will be a permanent position with McCall in Idaho. I don't know yet for sure."

"Get pregnant and you won't have to find out," her mother, the cold opportunist, said.

Because that worked out so well for you, she fired back in her head, but her mother was bitter enough at the world without her contributing to it.

"I'm not dating a billionaire, Mom." Her face had to be scarlet by now. She'd assured Dan she used contraceptives. What must he be thinking? "Sheriff McKillop is my boss. He was kidding around with a tabloid reporter and the joke went too far. Besides, I like my job. I worked hard to get where I am." *And not on my back, either.* Her mother tried to interrupt, but Jazz cut her off. "Look, I can't talk right now. I'm at work and I have a call on the other line. It's an emergency."

"Don't you dare hang up on me. I have more—"

Jazz disconnected midsentence and wriggled free of Dan's arms. Her shorts were in place. She tucked the phone in her back pocket. Her tank top was up next. It had gotten snagged on the spool of one wooden chair. She searched for her flip-flops, found them, and slid them onto her feet.

Dan leaned against the edge of the desk with arms folded across his chest and watched her. He wore a dark frown that didn't bode well.

They might as well get the unpleasantness over with. She'd known from the first that his money was going to be an issue. She hadn't had to defend herself for being her mother's daughter in years, but it was like riding a bicycle and experience kicked in.

"Go ahead and say what you're thinking," she invited him, bracing herself.

"You applied for a permanent position at McCall?"

Her bicycle riding experience was forgotten. She straightened to stare. "*That's* what you took away from that call?"

A slow, sexy, country star smile crinkled his eyes and his lips. "I didn't need a billion dollars for a pregnancy plot to unfold long before now. I'm not sure you're aware, but sheriffs make decent money. Plus, be honest. Even without any money at all, I'm quite a catch."

He was only trying to lighten the mood—whether for his benefit or hers she wasn't quite sure—but either way, he'd called it right. He was quite a catch. At the very least, he'd definitely make a serious contender for a sheriff's edition of *GQ* if they ever decided to run one. His uniform shirt was unbuttoned and his pants were unzipped, exposing the vee of darker hair on his flat belly that disappeared into his briefs. He'd slung his sidearm on the visitor chair. Rumpled blond hair and heated blue eyes alone guaranteed he'd make the cut.

Everything about this scene screamed how hot he was, and how hot she found him, considering her panties were on crooked and wedged into an uncomfortable bunch.

"Besides," he continued, "if I'd thought you were the type of woman who'd pull such a stunt, we wouldn't be where we are right now. I'd definitely have taken charge of the birth control, too."

She didn't know what he meant when he said *where we are right now.* The possibilities made her heart pound with a complex combination of emotions she didn't have time to examine in detail, but she did recognize her sense of relief.

Which, in itself, led to alarm.

"You don't know me," she said.

"I know enough." He drew her between his thighs, then cupped her face with his hands and gave her a series of soft, quick kisses that made her head spin and stole her breath for their sweetness. "If we're going to have our first fight, I'd rather it be about something important. When were you planning to tell me you're trying to get on at McCall?"

A first fight implied there'd be more. "Why would I tell you unless I'm offered the position? You're my boss," she pointed out, trying to think around his attempts to distract her.

"I hoped we were past that."

A pang of regret separated itself from the pack of emotions, stronger and deeper than expected, overriding that first rush of fear. They were slightly, although not completely, beyond it, and never would be, so there was no point in wishing for more. McCall aside, she wasn't about to subject him to her family. He had no idea what they were like. Since they wouldn't hesitate to ask him for money, it was best not to give them the chance. Her brother's contempt for the law wouldn't help Dan's career, either. He liked being sheriff or he wouldn't be planning to seek reelection.

"How far past that could we possibly get when I was only ever supposed to be here until October?"

Dan was quiet for far too long. Then, "I see," he said.

The disappointment on his face cut her heart. She hated that she'd put that look there, but it was definitely for the best that he understood she couldn't stay. How ironic was it, however, that her mother had spent her entire adult life in search of a man with money who'd stick around, and now that her daughter had found one who showed potential for being a keeper, she was the major reason why a real relationship between them would never gain any traction?

"No, you don't see," she said, and tried to explain. "You date women for short periods of time because you're looking to replace Andy, but so far you haven't found anyone who can. You'll be tired of me, too, in a few weeks, and then where will I be? Looking for a new job in a limited field? Do you have any idea how few positions for base managers there are, especially for women?"

"I don't even know how to begin to unwrap all of that." Dan lounged against his desk, his hands gripping the lip. "Let's start with Andy. Do you want me to tell you about her? Is she really all that important?"

"Yes, because she's important to you."

"She was." His jaw worked. "But as far as she was concerned, we were fuck buddies. That's it. She was a sharpshooter in the army and would look me up between deployments. Last year, she was killed in action."

Andy was dead. That explained why he'd claimed he no longer loved her.

Jazz's heart beat too fast and too hard. It pulsed in her ears. "Is there something about me that reminds you of her?" she asked quietly, and the guilty look in his eyes said it all, because of course there was. She was a firefighter. A smoke-jumper. She had a mild adrenaline addiction—the same as Andy, the sharpshooter, undoubtedly had. She'd set herself up to become his new fuck buddy, too.

"I'm not a booty call, Sheriff."

But yes.

Yes, she was.

She'd been so focused on his money that she'd dismissed the far deeper issue. She'd certainly misread his level of interest in her, and it stung.

The rain no longer pounded on the roof, so it should be safe enough for her to drive her bike back to the base. If not, she'd wait it out in the café and grab that coffee she so desperately needed. She searched for her purse. It peered out at her from under the table and she scooped it up.

"Hang on a second. You've made quite a few assumptions based on things other people told you, not me, and I never pegged you as a woman who listens to gossip," he said. "Yes, I like blond, leggy women. So does the entire male population of Grand, including my granddad. But I do not, under any circumstances, want to replace Andy. To a small-town boy, she was exciting. She was also exhausting, unpredictable, and more than a little unstable. I wondered about you at first, but other than the blond hair and long legs, you're nothing like her. I made damn sure of that before I took you skinny-dipping."

Deep down, Jazz wanted very much to believe him. However, she couldn't get past the nagging belief that good things never lasted. Not in her life, at least, and she found she couldn't do it—she couldn't become attached to him, only to have him grow bored and move on. Or, even worse, have one of her family members ask him for money, because then she'd have to kill them, and that would be awkward for him, since he was the sheriff.

"You're in luck," she said. "There are probably hundreds, if not thousands, of long-legged blonds in Montana who are nothing like her."

He rubbed the back of his neck. "That's not my point. They'd be nothing like you, either. I'm—"

This time, it was the shrill peal of his cell phone that interrupted.

✳

THE DOOR CLOSED behind Jazz before his phone even stopped ringing.

Dan would have ignored it—letting Jazz walk away without setting things right meant he might not get another opportunity—except his deputies only ever called his cell in an emergency.

He frowned at the door. She wasn't exhausting—far from it—but it didn't take a therapist to see how her mood had changed the second her mother called. "*Get pregnant and you won't have to find out.*"

What a role model. And yet Jazz had risen above it.

"What's up?" Dan growled into his phone, unable to rein in his frustration at the poorly timed interruption. The number belonged to Terry, his rookie.

"Chauncey O'Dell."

"Again, already?" This wasn't good. He began buttoning his shirt with one hand. Last time, Chauncey had waved a .223 caliber rifle at Terry, the new guy, and now Terry was skittish, so Dan had said he'd take the next call.

Every town had its mean drunk, and Chauncey was Grand's. Overall, he wasn't a bad guy. Then he'd have that one drink too many, take a swing at his wife, and one of the kids would call the sheriff's department to come sort it out. If Elaine would only press charges things would be simpler, but Dan was reluctant to override her and make a bad situation worse. She was the one who had to live with him. She might change her mind if Chauncey started going after the kids.

Dan had already decided not to let it get to that stage. He'd known Chauncey his whole life, and if Chauncey tried to wave a weapon at him, he'd arrest him on a whole different set of charges.

The O'Dells lived just outside of Grand on the opposite side of town from the road leading to the Endeavour. Their house wasn't exactly remote, but they ran beef cattle on several hundred acres of flatland so their neighbors weren't close.

Terry's car was already there. He'd parked at the end of the long drive and was waiting for Dan. The rain had stopped but the dirt drive was a slippery, mucky mess. Terry walked to Dan's window.

"No new activity," the deputy reported. His expression was worried. "No signs of life, either."

With any luck Chauncey had already passed out and his family had fled.

Dan called the house. Elaine answered, so there went that hope.

"Hey," he said. "The kids called. What's going on?"

"Nothing. Everything's fine."

She didn't sound fine. Her voice sounded strained. He drummed his thumb against the steering wheel while he mulled it over. The situation had a different feel to the ones in the past and he didn't like it.

"Calling the sheriff's department is serious business. Mind if I take a drive up to the house and have a word with the kids about that?"

There was a long stretch of silence that had his hackles rising. On the other end of the line, the house was too quiet. There were no background noises. No voices. No sounds of movement. Yet the boy had told Terry they were all home.

How did anyone keep a five-year-old, a six-year-old, and an eight-year-old silent?

"Don't put yourself out. I'll speak to them," Elaine said. And Dan heard the fear.

"No trouble at all."

He hung up the phone without giving her a chance to answer and started the engine. He leaned through his open window. "I'm driving up to the house," he said to Terry.

"You stay here and wait for me."

Long grass waved at him from either side of the drive. Mud splashed against the underside of his SUV. He passed a red barn on his right that had seen better days. It looked like a fun place to play. Maybe the kids were in there.

The house at the end of the drive was an old, two-story log home that someone had desecrated with gray vinyl siding. He pulled up in front of the sagging porch and got out. He walked around the hood of his SUV, mud sucking at his boots.

And there was Chauncey in the doorway, waving that damned .223 around as if it were some sort of flyswatter. The fool.

"I believe my wife told you we don't need you here," Chauncey said mildly. "That means you're trespassing, Dan. I'll give you ten seconds to get back in your vehicle and get out."

"I just came to talk," Dan replied.

Chauncey pointed the rifle at him. "You the man been sleeping with my wife?"

Now, Dan was pissed. "No, I'm not sleeping with your wife, and put down that damned rifle. Don't make me have to take you in. I hate the paperwork involved," he said sharply.

"Man's got a right to defend his property against tres-passers, Sheriff. 'Specially if the trespasser's armed."

Chauncey weaved a bit on his feet, giving Dan a much

better idea of how drunk he was and how much trouble Dan might be in. All he could think of, however, was, *where are the kids?*

He put his hands in the air. "My gun's in its holster."

Chauncey flicked off the safety and they passed the point of no return as far as good outcomes were concerned. "Time's up."

The scene shifted to slow motion even as Dan's thought processes revved, considering his options.

There was a slight movement behind Chauncey. Dan caught sight of Elaine with a cast iron frying pan gripped in both hands. She swung it at the back of Chauncey's head, putting all her weight behind it, which sadly, wasn't much.

The rifle went off. Its punch took Dan's left leg out from beneath him. He landed on his side in the mud, then instinct had him rolling for cover under his SUV. He clawed at his holster, trying to get his gun free.

He knew he was bleeding. He could feel the spreading puddle of warmth. But he got why Jazz liked adrenaline so much, because so far, he was feeling no pain. The crash would be coming, however.

Chauncey had turned on his wife, who looked small and afraid as she faced him, and he raised the butt of his rifle, looking angry enough to use it on her. Dan heard the fast-approaching roar of an engine. That had to be Terry, inexperienced, riding a rescue mission straight into a disaster Dan had created, all because he'd underestimated a drunk. A quick decision was called for before someone was killed.

His gun hand was unsteady, leaving him afraid he might hit Elaine by mistake. He had to get Chauncey far enough away from her that she wasn't at risk.

"Hey, Chauncey," he shouted. "Drop your weapon. You're under arrest."

Chauncey spun toward Dan, and Dan saw the face of a man who'd been scared sober and believed he now had nothing to lose. If Dan didn't stop him there'd be four bodies for his deputies to collect at the end of the day, because Chauncey would take Dan, Elaine, and Terry with him. That assessment didn't even factor in the three missing kids.

Where are the kids?

Dan's vision swam as he lined up his shot. He fired, hitting Chauncey in the chest.

Chauncey's legs folded. He sagged to his knees, dropping the rifle.

✳

DAN OPENED HIS eyes. He scraped at his tongue with his teeth. Aftereffects of the anesthetic left it furry.

Dallas lounged in the chair next to his hospital bed, spooning green hospital gelatin into his mouth. "Great. You're awake." He dropped the empty plastic cup and spoon on the bedside tray.

"How can you eat that stuff?" Dan asked, eyeing his friend with disgust.

Dallas poured ice water from a sweaty pitcher into another small plastic cup. "I ate a ton of it during my residency, trying to convince little kids it's better than ice cream. Eventually, you buy into the lie." He passed Dan the cup of water. "Sip it slowly. How do you feel?"

"Not too bad, all things considered." Dan looked around. "What happened to Ryan?" He vaguely recalled him being in the room at one point.

"Gone to pick up Jazz. After I pumped you full of Demerol you became quite insistent you wanted to see her, but ranted on and on about no one letting her drive to the hospital on her motorcycle. It was pretty funny. You have crap tolerance for morphine, by the way."

"Great." He really did want to see Jazz, so he supposed he could have made far worse demands.

Dallas shifted into doctor mode. "The bullet struck the femoral artery in your left thigh. It was a solid point bullet, so lucky for you it was clean in and out, but you lost a lot of blood and they had to give you a transfusion. Your deputy saved you from bleeding to death, by the way. He has excellent first aid training. You owe him a big Christmas bonus. And your parents are in the waiting room. Your mom seems pretty mad at you, so you've been warned."

"What about the kids?" Dan asked, suddenly anxious. He'd passed out before finding out what happened to them.

"The kids are fine. The oldest boy kept the two younger ones hidden in the field behind the house. Their mother has taken them to Marietta to be with her parents."

Dallas gave him a quick rundown of everything that happened after the ambulance arrived. Dan had been rushed to the small local hospital in Grand where Dallas had been on call. Dallas determined the need for a vascular surgeon, so he'd had Dan transported to Billings.

"Chauncey O'Dell is under guard in the ICU. He's going to live," he finished. "I doubt if that makes him too happy."

"I don't give a damn if the bastard's happy or not." Guilt washed over Dan. Never again would he allow a woman to make the final decision as to when she'd had enough of an abusive relationship.

But, while he'd made a mess of the situation, at the same time, his gut told him if he hadn't taken the call, he'd be a deputy short and those kids would no longer have a mother.

Speaking of mothers...

Dan's mom eased open the door, saw he was awake, and then spent the next half hour alternately hugging and swearing at him.

Chapter Twelve

MIDNIGHT HAD SLID past by the time Jazz arrived. Visiting hours were long gone as well, but Ryan had taken care of that minor detail.

She'd left Eli monitoring the team in California for her, which didn't feel right, but Dan had asked for her. She'd had no choice but to come. She'd had to see for herself that he was okay, because Ryan's reassurances hadn't been nearly enough.

Their last conversation replayed in her head, stuck on repeat. She'd walked out without so much as saying goodbye. What if that turned out to be her last memory of him?

Could she have lived with it?

She didn't plan to disturb him if he was asleep. Ryan had said the pain medication had left him "pretty loopy." When she pushed open the door to his hospital room, however, she found him wide awake and counting the tiles on the ceiling.

The dimmed lights left much of the small private room soaked in shadow. Dan, however, propped up on pillows, was plain to see. Her heart gripped her lungs. His ruffled blond hair spiked in the front. He had the white cotton blanket pulled up to his waist, so she couldn't see any bandages, but the hospital gown drawn tight across his broad chest drummed home to her how lucky he was to be alive.

"Hey," she said softly. There was something about a hospital at night that made anything above a whisper sound sacrilegious. "Did someone in here place a booty call?"

Dan's low, heated chuckle seared straight through her. "I did promise you that we'd try this in a bed, didn't I?"

"You didn't have to go to all of this trouble on my account."

She tiptoed across the room to a beige, vinyl armchair that had already been drawn up beside him. She reached for his hand. It was warm and strong, and he laced his fingers through hers. The backs of her eyes prickled. He could have been killed and his final memory of her would have been that she'd picked a fight.

She squeezed his hand tight. "I'm really angry with you."

Dan squeezed back. Blue eyes met hers. "I don't know how to make it any plainer to you that what I once had with Andy has nothing to do with what's happening between you and me now."

"That's not why I'm angry." She warmed to her topic, allowing all of the fear from the moment Ryan had arrived at the base with the news that he'd been shot to spill over. "How dare you complain about my motorcycle, then turn around and approach a drunk armed with a rifle when you aren't wearing body armor?"

"I didn't think he'd actually shoot me," he said.

"What did you think an armed man might do? Didn't you learn anything about risk management in sheriff school?"

His lips twitched at that. "Sheriff school, huh? Mostly, they teach us how to manage budgets and eat donuts. But I'll make you a deal. I'll wear my body armor from now on if you'll wear your helmet, even if it's only to the end of the driveway."

"Deal."

"Still angry with me?"

"Not quite as much." She'd never been angry.

She'd been afraid. And while that did make her angry, it wasn't with him. It was because she disliked feeling so helpless. She was used to being in the thick of the action, not sitting things out on the sidelines.

"Good. Then I want to talk about what happened this afternoon," he said.

"You've got to be kidding me. This isn't really a booty call, Dan. What is it with men? Besides, Ryan already warned me it will be a few weeks before you're fully"—she ran her gaze to his hips, then back to his eyes, raising her brows—"functional again."

"You might want to consider the source of that bit of information. Trust me. I'm fully functional this very second." He shifted his weight as if trying to find a more comfortable position, although the slight grimace suggested he wasn't having much luck. "But that's not what I want to talk about."

"If it's about McCall," she said warily, knowing it probably wasn't, "I really want that job." Because he deserved so much better than the trouble she'd bring if she stayed in Grand too much longer.

The hint of a smile flickered on his face. "I know you do. And I get it. It's a great career opportunity. But let's set that aside for later, too. Tell me about your mother. While she seems very eager for grandchildren, I'm sensing you don't have a warm and loving relationship with her."

Jazz tried to picture her mother with grandchildren and failed. Talking about her always left her on edge, but he might as well know what he was up against. He'd already figured most of it out. She rubbed her thumb against the side of his palm while she collected her thoughts and her courage, then took a deep breath and let it all out.

"That's quite the understatement, Sheriff. My mother is an alcoholic with substance abuse and gambling issues. She's been in and out of rehab for as long as I can remember. I have two half brothers. I was eight when the oldest was born. I doubt if she has the slightest idea of who our fathers might be. I certainly don't. I raised both boys from babies because she was never around. I haven't seen them since I left home twelve years ago, which makes me no better than her as far as abandonment goes. Leo is now twenty. He seems to be doing okay for himself. The twenty-two-year-old, Todd, takes after our mother. He's good-looking and he uses that to his advantage. He has a massive sense of entitlement and zero respect for women or the law. I don't hear from any of them unless they want money. I call them on birthdays and holidays. Other than that, they don't hear from me at all."

And yet she couldn't escape them. She was their bankroll. She shuddered to think of the demands they'd make on Dan if they believed they could use her relationship with him to their advantage.

Rubber-soled footsteps squeaked outside the door, paused for a moment, then moved on. Dan's attention remained focused on her.

"My family must seem so different to you," he said.

"They're wonderful." Dan could keep his billions. She cared nothing for money. His family, however?

That was definitely something she envied.

"They're hardly perfect, Jazz. If Grand were a big city, my father and grandfather would be slum lords. They'll pinch a penny until it begs for mercy. My sisters are jealous of each other. They show up at family events to see which one of them has gained the most weight and whose kids are doing better in school. And, in case you're wondering, they all hit me up for money on a regular basis. Thanks to those fancy sheriff school budgeting lessons though, I've learned how to say no."

He really had no idea, although it was sweet that he thought he did. "How many family members have you bailed out of jail?" she asked.

"None, so far." His eyes twinkled. "But you've met my nieces and nephews. It's only a matter of time."

"Have any of them ever shoplifted groceries to feed two younger brothers? Or buy Christmas and birthday presents for them?" It wasn't something she was proud of, but it was either that or let Child and Family Services take the boys away. She knew other kids who'd been in and out of protective custody, and the stories they told had made her shoplifting worthwhile. And, truth be told, she'd gotten a bit of a rush from the danger involved. She'd liked the feeling, even back then. "What about sitting up all night with their mother so she doesn't choke to death on her vomit?"

The twinkle in his eyes disappeared. "I get it. Your mother is a weak human being. On the other hand, you most definitely are not. And if you think I'd judge a little girl for doing what she had to in order to survive, then you're insulting me. I care most about who you are right now, and from where I sit, you're pretty remarkable."

She was proud of the things she'd accomplished, but she wasn't special. "Lots of people come from worse backgrounds than mine and do okay for themselves."

"And lots of them fail. People come from better backgrounds than mine, too, and fall on their asses. Nine times out of ten, success is about the person. Some people need a break. Some people make their own." Dan didn't take his eyes off of hers. "You should talk to Ryan."

"About success?"

"About his childhood. If he wants to tell you about it, he will. It's not my story. But let's just say, his makes yours look like a Disney movie."

She swallowed, but the hard, painful lump in her throat didn't budge. She didn't need to talk to Ryan about whose childhood was shittier because it didn't matter. She'd simply wanted Dan to understand why she should never have begun things with him in the first place.

She hated seeing him in that bed. She hated the fine lines of pain around his eyes and pinching his mouth. She hated that he might have died. But not as much as she hated the thought of him ever coming to hate her because she couldn't shake off her family. She hadn't been able to see them starve when she was a child and she couldn't let them go hungry now that she was an adult. She didn't have much to give them, but what she did give was all hers. It would stay that way, too.

"I'm not in competition with Ryan over who had it worse," she said. Her voice came out raspy and wobbled a bit. "I'm here because I had to see for myself that you're okay. But this isn't working for me." She tried to clear her throat and failed again. "I have a crew in a wildfire in California and I should be monitoring them, not here with you." She shook her hand free of Dan's and pried herself out of the ugly, uncomfortable hospital chair. She forced herself to stand straight and speak with a conviction she was far from feeling. "I don't think we should see each other, anymore. If you need reports from the base between now and October, from now on you can get them from Eli."

＊

RYAN WAS ON standby, waiting in the main lobby to drive Jazz back to the base. She'd stopped in the ladies' room first to have a good cry. If he had an opinion regarding her red eyes and blotchy skin, he kept it to himself.

They made the first half of the two-hour drive from Billings to Grand without speaking. Jazz burrowed into the Mercedes' butter-yellow, soft leather seats and would have been happy to complete the entire trip the same way, but around the halfway mark, Ryan wanted to chat. It was creeping on toward four in the morning and the road ahead, a dark tunnel rimmed by off-ramp lighting, was mostly empty.

"Did Dan ever tell you how he, Dallie, and I became friends?" he asked, his eyes on the road. He didn't wait for an answer. "We lived in the same residence our first year at Montana State. We took an economics class together and shared an assignment. Dan and Dallie were both small-town boys and I introduced them to city nightlife. I'd been running the streets for about nine years by that time and there's always places to drink, no matter how old—or young—you are. Dan was already interested in law enforcement, although more from morbid curiosity, I think. He had a wild streak, a sense of adventure, steady nerves, and if he hadn't had such a strong family base, could have gone either way. He was real protective of his friends. Dallie would try anything once. He just liked having fun."

He cast a quick glance her way, checking to see if she was listening.

She was all ears.

"Dallie was easy to read," he continued. "What you see is what you get. Dan was the challenge. I wanted to be friends with him so bad, but I didn't trust him not to turn on me. So, when we were out drinking one night, I put him to the test. We'd had a few, but didn't really have enough money on us to get drunk, and we were walking back to our residence because we didn't have bus fare. We passed a convenience store. A cop had left his keys in his cruiser while he was inside the store, because who would steal a cop car, right?"

He shot her another look. She was still listening. And she could already see where this story was going.

"I hopped in the driver's seat and told them both to get in. Dallie didn't have to think twice. He was curious as to what would happen next. Dan, though… He didn't approve. You could see it on his face. I slammed the door and would have driven off without him, and when he realized I was going to leave and take Dallie with me, he jumped in the back."

The dashboard light caught the slight smile that the memory evoked.

"It didn't take long for the police to set up a road block. I wasn't interested in avoiding them, anyway. It wasn't the first time I'd been arrested, but it was a first for Dallie and Dan, and I wanted to see how they'd deal with it. Who they'd blame."

"Let me guess. They owned their share of it," Jazz said. Ryan wasn't the only reformed juvenile delinquent in the car. She'd run with kids like him and knew the value they placed on loyalty and trust. She valued those things, herself. And yet she didn't believe he'd been a street kid by necessity—rather, he'd been one by choice.

What kind of person chose that kind of life?

He nodded. "They did. And the judge went easy on us because they were honest and had clean records. Dan kicked my ass for it, though. Then he told me I could screw up my own life if that's what I wanted, but he and Dallie had plans for theirs and if I ever did something like that again, he'd cut me loose." That smile flashed again, brighter this time. "He didn't care all that much about me stealing the cruiser. He figured if the cop was dumb enough to leave his keys in it, he got what he deserved. But he continues to lecture me on the dangers of drinking and driving to this day."

That sounded like Dan.

A part of her hungered for Ryan to tell her more about him. Her practical side warned she should just let it go and move on. She'd made her choice. She didn't get to have it both ways.

The look on Dan's face...

She relived his disappointment in her whenever she closed her eyes. All she wanted right now was to climb into bed and nurse her sore heart.

"Is there a point to this story?" she asked.

Ryan pulled the Mercedes out and passed a car that kept straying a little too far into the left-hand lane, as if its driver might be having difficulty staying awake.

"Yes. Dan's been hurt by one woman already. I'd hate to see him get hurt again."

She wondered if that was a threat. It had the feel of one, considering the source, and Ryan gave the impression of someone who'd have no problem carrying it through. She wasn't easily intimidated, however. Besides, her status with Dan was none of his business.

"You give me too much credit," she said.

"I'm giving all the credit to Dan. I know him. If he cares about you, and I think he does, he'll stand by you no matter how damaging your connections might be to him."

She processed his words. It took her a second. Then, rage blistered inside her as she figured it out. "You had me investigated."

He didn't deny it. "I like you, Jazz. You're okay. But your brothers are thugs. Todd lives off hard-working wom-en, then gets rough with them if they complain. You know that already, though, because you've bailed him out of jail a few times. But did you know Leo's an off-the-books debt collector for a few of the casinos? I'm guessing you don't."

Disappointment in Leo mingled with her rage over Ryan's high-handedness. She'd had hopes for her youngest brother. No wonder he quit asking for money. Then, guilt chased the disappointment away. He'd had no one to guide him, to help him make better life choices, and she'd let him down. She should have been there for him.

"And your mother." Ryan was shaking his head. "She's something else. She sued three different men over your paternity and still couldn't come up with a winner. Did you know she did hit one for Leo? Rehab's expensive, though. I'd imagine she's getting desperate for money again, now that Leo's an adult and the child support payments have stopped."

Her face was so hot she feared her cheeks might split open. There was nothing like having her secrets tossed out and dissected with such clinical detachment. "You're an asshole."

"I really am," he said frankly, not at all bothered by her opinion of him. "There's no point in playing games with each other, so here's the deal. Dan wants you, but he doesn't need your family, too. How much would it cost me to make them go away?"

The nerve was breathtaking. She squinted at him. "Are you trying to *bribe* me?"

"God, no." Ryan's dark eyes went almost comically wide. "I'm trying to help Dan. You're acting like somebody died. Since I took on over four hours of driving because he was desperate to see you, and I got three texts while you were in the washroom telling me to make sure you're okay, if something went wrong between you, it must be your fault. Face it, Jazz. Dan's the best guy you're ever going to meet. Your family is pretty much the only sticking point that I've found. I can fix that. Then you can both be happy."

Jazz massaged her eyes with her fingers. She was tired, she was upset, and inclined to become giddy over the ridiculous turn this conversation had taken. As far as Ryan was concerned, whatever Dan wanted, he was going to get. "*His makes yours look like a Disney movie,*" Dan had said about Ryan's childhood.

The giddiness grew worse. "I'm not a commodity. You can't buy me," she said.

"But I can buy off your family. Am I right?"

As much as she hated to admit it, he wasn't wrong. "They'd be back as soon as the money runs out." She spoke from experience.

"No, they wouldn't."

His hands were relaxed on the leather-wrapped steering wheel. His face reflected a sinister calm that gave her the creeps. He was like Dr. Jekyll and Mr. Hyde—reasonable and sane one moment, then all of a sudden, scary as hell. She might be better off taking her chances on the side of the

183

highway at four o'clock in the morning than driving any farther with him. Who knew where she'd end up? Only his friendship with Dan kept her from demanding he stop the car and let her get out.

"There's no need to buy off my family," she said. "I'm here until October. Then I'm gone."

"Are you sure about that? You could have a permanent job in Grand if you wanted it. You're a firefighter. The town would hire you. And every season, the base manager position would be yours again. You've earned it."

"I don't need Grand. I have a job in Helena and I've applied for a permanent position at McCall."

"McCall is already a well-established training base. I can't see you spending the next thirty or forty years riding on someone else's achievements. Where's the challenge in that? Why not give McCall a run for its money and turn Custer County into the best training base in the country? Then, the credit's all yours."

It bothered her that Ryan had figured out the challenge McCall posed was a large part of what had made her apply for that position. It bothered her even more that she was tempted by the alternative he offered.

The sign for the turnoff to Grand leaped out from the tunnel of darkness ahead. In a few minutes, she'd be home. No, that was wrong. The base wasn't home—it was more of a haven. Home was a place she'd only ever tried to escape from, not to.

And yet it continued to find her. Even worse, if what she suspected was true, then her family had attracted the attention of something far bigger and a great deal more ruthless. The O'Reillys were little more than petty thieves—grifters, at best. Ryan's family, on the other hand…

Dan, what have you gotten yourself into?

"I'll think about it," she lied.

Chapter Thirteen

D**AN HAD BEEN** on the fence about his living room already. Spending idle hours with his leg propped on pillows while his mother fussed over him, and staring at the art-laden walls, made him hate it. The landscapes he was okay with, but the carved wooden buffalo on the mantel was too cliché for words.

As for the vases of flowers, there'd been plenty of those before he'd been shot. He could open his own floral shop now.

His bad mood had nothing to do with the décor—well, not a whole lot—and everything to do with the fact that Jazz still hadn't made an appearance.

Her concern for him hadn't been fake. She'd arrived at midnight to see him. She'd clung tightly to his hand at the hospital. He'd been certain that, after a few days to think about things, she'd be on his doorstep, willing to talk.

But he'd spent a week in the hospital, and now, two days at home. That was nine days in total. He'd give it another day or two of physiotherapy so he'd be more mobile, and then he'd go to her. If all that kept her from exploring where things between them might go was a family of freeloaders, then she didn't give him enough credit.

He heard the main doorbell, suffered a brief leap of hope, then dialed it back to reality. His mother was screening his visitors, refusing to allow sheriff or ranch business to intrude on his recovery. If it was Jazz though, she'd let her in.

His mother marched into the living room from the kitchen, which she'd claimed as her own, wiping her hands on a towel. "Don't move," she ordered him on her way past, as if afraid he might leap off the sofa and make a break for freedom when she opened the door.

He heard a female voice, too far away to identify, then two sets of footsteps. Optimism leaped in his chest as the main door to his living room opened.

"You have a visitor," his mother said, stepping aside to allow a woman—who wasn't Jazz—to enter first.

Dan's flash of disappointment quickly shifted to interest. The woman was tall, blond, and lovely. Exceedingly so. Jaw dropping, in fact. High heels and tight jeans made her legs appear that much longer. A plain white blouse was tucked in at the front. Long sleeves covered her arms. She looked too much like Jazz for there not to be a connection. Her age was difficult to guess because she'd had a few nips and tucks, but since Jazz didn't have an older sister, he was going to place her around fifty. She was softer than Jazz, with less muscle mass, but she'd have to work out to stay in this kind of shape.

This was what Jazz would look like in twenty or so years—except for the cosmetic surgery, of course. That, he couldn't imagine.

She crossed the room with confidence and grace, her hand extended, a bright smile fixed firmly in place. "I'm so happy to finally meet you. I'm Keira, Jasmine's mother."

At first glance, no one would ever believe that this beautiful, confident, and sexy—she moved in a way guaranteed to make sure men noticed—woman would encourage her daughter to get pregnant in order to snag a man with money. Her smile brimmed with a warmth that spilled into her eyes. Eyes were a tell.

But as she'd first walked through the door, she'd checked out the room before looking at him. She'd forgotten his mother, too, which didn't earn her any points as far as he was concerned, and since her approval rating had started off shaky, she was already fighting uphill. All he had to do was picture a twelve-year-old Jazz stealing food to feed two little boys and the strikes were against her.

He shook the hand she offered him and prepared to be dazzled. This show should be good.

"Mrs. O'Reilly," he said, just to get under her skin, because as far as he knew from what Jazz had said, there was no Mr. O'Reilly and never had been. "I've heard a lot about you."

Her laugh was like the tinkle of crystal wind chimes

stirred by a light summer breeze. "Call me Keira. And I'm sure none of it was good. Jasmine was never a mommy's girl by any stretch of the imagination. The fights we had… What a handful to raise!"

Dan didn't doubt it. Jazz would have her own ideas about right and wrong. Probably better ones, too. He invited Kiera to sit. His mother offered her coffee.

"Bring a cup for yourself too," he said to his mother. He'd be curious to hear her impression of Keira later.

Keira settled into the wingback chair closest to Dan. "I heard about your accident and had to come. Jasmine never lets on when she's upset, but a mother knows these things." She glanced at his mother and offered her another one of those charming smiles. "Do you have any daughters?"

"Two."

"Then you understand."

Ordinarily, Freda McKillop was nobody's fool, but Dan could see her falling for Keira's act. She automatically assumed every mother loved her children, even if some were better at showing it than others. She likely thought Keira was simply unorthodox.

She was certainly that. In Dan's mind, however, she was already ticking the boxes for narcissistic, passive-aggressive behavior. She'd started off by playing the victim—Jazz was a handful. Jazz didn't communicate… If he hadn't overheard that phone conversation between them, it might have taken him longer to catch on himself. Signs of a drug problem were there too, although they weren't conclusive. Long sleeves on a hot day. The whites of her eyes were shot through with red and she kept her hands busy to hide a slight tremor.

His mother went to check on the coffee.

"You have two sisters, so you know how stubborn women can be," Keira said to him.

Did he ever. He wasn't stupid enough to say that out loud with his mother in hearing range though, so he made a noise that could be interpreted any number of ways.

"Jasmine can be especially stubborn. She's always been fearless, too," her mother continued. "It's no surprise she decided to become a firefighter. It's certainly no surprise to me that she's fallen for a sheriff, either."

"She likes my guns," Dan said, straight-faced.

Jazz's mother wasn't stupid. She also knew how to flirt. "I'm sure she does," she replied, arching one brow. Her eyes sparkled. "She's always had a weakness for bull riders, too. Their guns are especially impressive."

He'd brought that one on himself.

Dan's mother had returned with a tray filled with cups of coffee, cream, and sugar. She'd added a plate of home-baked chocolate chip cookies. His favorite.

"Your daughter is lovely," she said.

Keira beamed. "Thank you." She accepted a cup of coffee but refused cream and sugar. She passed on the cookies, too. "As a concerned mother, I couldn't leave Grand without meeting the man who's finally captured my daughter's affections. I want to thank you, Dan. I was beginning to think I might never have grandchildren."

Dan's mother's face was a study of conflict. She'd met Jazz all of once, so talk of grandchildren had to seem premature. He could pinpoint the exact instant she began wondering whether or not he'd been holding out on her. If he didn't move this performance along, he could kiss the rest of those cookies goodbye.

"No need to thank me," he said to Keira. "Jazz is only here for another month or so. She's more interested in her career than in babies anyway, and I can't say I'm too fond of kids either. The real fun's been in the trying."

Both mothers looked appropriately shocked by that statement, although his mom somewhat more so. He'd been raised to treat women with respect. His older sisters had beaten that into him at an early age. And as far as him not liking kids?

That would be news to his nieces and nephews.

"Jasmine is hardly the type of girl to sleep around," Keira said, her shock quite convincing.

"She could have fooled me," he replied.

"*Dan!*" His mother's sharp tone left no question regarding her shock whatsoever.

"A guy's got to be careful with his money. Jazz knows where we stand."

Keira gave up on the motherly angle and went for a more practical, business approach. She regarded him coolly. "A girl's got to look after herself, too. You're her boss. If there's an understanding between you, then she should be compensated for her time, don't you agree?"

"You mean like a bonus?" Although in legal circles it might be called something else. Either way, his curiosity about Jazz's mother was satisfied. He was done. "I'm not responsible for Jazz's paycheck, Mrs. O'Reilly. I provide the facilities for the smokejumper base. She's not my employee."

"I see." The porcelain coffee cup clattered onto a glass side table. Pink lipstick smirched its white rim. "I'm sorry there's no time for us to get to know each other better, but I have a plane to catch. It was lovely to meet you both." Her smile encompassed his mother, too, although it no longer reached her eyes. "I wish you well with your recovery, Dan."

His mother rose, too. "I'll see you out."

He couldn't help drawing comparisons between the two women as they walked from the room. Freda McKillop was probably only ten years older than Keira O'Reilly, but she could easily pass for her mother. Her long hair was gray, her body had grown soft, her clothes weren't stylish even though she could afford better, and what was more, she didn't care. As far as Dan could tell, his dad didn't care either. She'd spent the past few days making Dan all of his favorite foods and fussing over him in general. He was her baby and he kind of liked it.

Best of all, never once had she tried to pimp him out. Jazz was right. His family was wonderful and he'd have them no other way.

Jazz was wonderful, too. It was a shame her own family didn't appreciate it.

His mother returned alone. She planted her hands on her hips. Her expression was thundercloud black.

"I should probably explain what that was all about," he said, suddenly wary.

"You don't have to." She stared hard at the door she'd just closed as if willing it to spontaneously combust. "That woman is some piece of work."

He might as well break the news to her now. He locked his fingers behind his head, shifted his leg into a more comfortable position on the pillows, and spoke to the wide wooden beams on the ceiling. "That woman is going to be my mother-in-law, someday."

His mother's lightning-filled eyes trickled sparks as she swiveled to gape. "*Seriously?*"

"Seriously." Although he had his work cut out for him as far as convincing Jazz of it went. She had no idea how real relationships worked and that she could share her problems with him. She was as stunted as Ryan in that regard—they both had massive trust issues.

The storm clouds dissipated. His mother beamed from ear to ear. "Perfect. I won't have to worry about sharing you at Christmas."

✳

JAZZ HADN'T YET decided whether or not she should talk to Dan about Ryan. She'd been too busy to give it the thought it deserved. That didn't mean she wasn't worried—only that she had other things on her mind, too.

Her team had returned from Southern California and she'd received ego-stoking praise for her input to their operations plan. She'd been tasked with writing recommendations for procedural changes based on her input, as well as drafting a new operations plan for a small fire currently under watch in Montana's Swan Range. Her new plan had to incorporate protection measures for the habitat corridor of the local grizzly population, because grizzlies were considered an endangered species, although she was more worried about ensuring protection for her team, who were on standby. If they were called in, they'd be working the slopes. Fire moved faster uphill and current weather conditions were a cause for concern. The possibility of missing even one potential safety hazard had her on edge.

She was alone in her office and buried in research when Dan hobbled in on crutches. He wore khaki cargo shorts, loafers, and a black cotton, Custer County Sheriff's T-shirt embossed with gold print. She didn't care that he was supposed to be dealing with Eli from now on.

"What are you doing here?" she cried, jumping to her feet. "You're supposed to be at home, resting!"

He propped the crutches against the wall and allowed her to help ease him into a chair. Soap, spicy aftershave, and the aroma of chocolate chip cookies tickled her nose. He felt warm, solid, and thankfully, alive. A flutter in her belly made her feel alive, too.

She'd missed him.

He held up a small brown paper bag with a grease stain on the bottom. "My mom sent you cookies. I said I'd deliver them."

"Your mom sent me cookies?" Her heart did a happy little dance of surprise. She reached for them.

He tucked them behind his back. "Not so fast. They're a bribe."

She straightened. "Your mom is trying to bribe me?" If so, it turned out—given the right currency—she could be bought, after all.

He looked around. "Is there an echo in here?"

"Funny. What does your mother want from me?"

"She wants you to come to dinner. And before you comment on that, yes, she's fixated on feeding people, too. Especially people she likes. Get a few of her meals under your belt and Brody will have no problem beating your times on that obstacle course."

Jazz tried not to read too much into Dan's mother's invitation. From what she'd seen, Freda was friendly with everyone in Grand. She was also as intent as Ryan when it came to getting Dan something he wanted. When had Jazz turned into a prize?

"I can't," she said. But she wanted to. And Dan sensed it.

"You have to. You owe her. Your mother dropped in for a visit the other day and she hasn't yet recovered from the shock."

She must be stupid because she didn't get what he meant. She had no idea what he was talking about. "My mother's in Vegas."

Dan's blond eyebrows connected. "You didn't know she was here?"

Her stomach hit bottom. There was only one reason why she'd come to Grand. "Tell me she didn't ask you for money."

"Not for herself. She told me I should pay you a bonus for sleeping with me, though."

Jazz closed her eyes. Mortification scorched her whole body and seared the backs of her lids. "I'll kill her."

"That's probably not the right thing to say in front of a sheriff," he said. "Besides, my mom is the one who was surprised by the request, not me. I don't mind paying you to sleep with me if it means it'll happen more often." His expression sobered. "I'm sorry. I didn't realize your mother hadn't dropped in on you, too."

Nothing her mother did surprised her anymore. She didn't want or need pity. "Why would she? I don't have your kind of money." Although whoever she'd borrowed travel fare from would eventually need to be paid back, so she'd hear from her then. "But how, precisely, did my sleeping with you come up in conversation with our *mothers*?"

"She thanked me for taking you off her hands and giving her the opportunity to finally become a grandmother. I didn't want to get anyone's hopes up about grandchildren though, so I pointed out that you're only interested in me for sex. I might have insinuated you're easy."

She didn't especially care what her mother thought, since she had no right to judge, but their sex life wasn't something she wanted discussed with his mother. "This is all a big joke to you, isn't it?"

His eyes, so warm and blue, shimmered with heat. "No, Jazz, it's not. But face it. Your mother is only as much a part of your life as you allow her to be."

Anger bubbled up and boiled over. Frustration, too. Because that was easy for him to say. His mother baked cookies. She invited people into her home because she liked them, not to get what she could out of them. He'd never have to turn his back on her, because she'd never give him a reason to. She would never turn her back on him, either.

Jazz's family, on the other hand, wasn't large and noisy and close. They didn't particularly like each other all that much. None of them were very reliable, and that included herself. She'd let her brothers down—Leo in particular—by leaving Las Vegas. But if she didn't care what happened to them, then nobody would. How sad was that?

"She's as much a part of my life as I decide I can live with," she said.

"She can be as much a part of my life as I decide I can

live with too, then," he replied calmly. "The same goes for you and my mother. She'll run your life if you let her." He grinned at her, and Jazz's heart fluttered. "There. Now we've both been warned. See how easy that was?"

"Not so fast." If she was going to say something about that drive home from Billings, now was the time. "Ryan and I had a long talk on the car ride from the hospital. He believes my family will hurt your chances for reelection. Then he offered to pay them to stay away from you."

"I'll talk to him," Dan said. "He can be overprotective sometimes."

Dan didn't sound nearly as alarmed by that as he should. There had barely been a fraction of a second of hesitation before his response.

"That's it? He can be overprotective?"

A longer pause said he was choosing his next words with a great deal more care. "Ryan doesn't let many people get close to him. You of all people should understand that. You both worry too much, too." His lips tightened, ever so slightly, as he slipped into Sheriff Dan mode. "No one's paying anyone to stay away from me, Jazz. If word of that got out, believe me, it would be a bigger blow to my reelection campaign than either one of your warped family trees."

"Ryan's family tree doesn't worry you either?"

"Not in the least. He hasn't had any contact with his family since he was a kid."

Dan sounded so sure of it. She hoped he was right. "And

it doesn't bother you that he thinks mine is more objectionable than his?"

"He doesn't think that. He thinks your family has a tighter grip on you, that's all. I'm inclined to agree. You took on responsibility for all of them, including your mother, when you were too young to know what the word meant. You don't know how to let go of it, either. But you wouldn't be who you are if you did. It's what makes you such a good base manager. You need to work on those trust issues, though. And you might want to let people think for themselves, too." He held up the paper bag. "Do you want these cookies or not?"

She eyed the bag. She'd been honest with him. He'd met her mother, so he'd seen the proof. If he wasn't worried, then at least her conscience was clear on that score. The ache she'd had in her chest ever since saying goodbye to him the night at the hospital finally let go. She even dared to let herself think that starting a training base in Grand might be worth considering, after all.

She plucked the bag from his hand before he could hide it again. She peered inside. A dozen or more cookies, soft, plump, and loaded with chocolate chips, beamed back. She took one, bit into its fat, sweet gooeyness, and offered the bag to Dan so he could help himself, too.

"When's dinner?" she asked.

Chapter Fourteen

DAN PROPPED HIS stiff leg on the sectional sofa facing Ryan's office in the common room that joined their private homes.

He wasn't quite as offhand about his friend's interference as he'd let on to Jazz. Something was eating at Ryan and a team meeting seemed the best way to sound him out. They were long overdue for one, anyway. Between his job, Jazz, and getting shot, he'd lost track of what his best friends were up to in their personal lives.

Ryan sat next to him in an overstuffed chair. Dallie parked himself at the bend in the sectional, but only after satisfying himself that Dan hadn't done any damage to his leg by driving himself to the base.

"I'm good with having a personal physician," Dan said, slapping Dallas's probing fingers away, "but I've gotta be honest. You always checking my junk the second you walk into the room is freaking me out."

"I don't care what women tell you. Your junk is nothing special," Dallie replied. "I only have to look down to see the real deal."

"Why do doctors have such huge egos?" Ryan mused to himself.

Dallas flipped his shaggy curls out of his eyes. He was in need of a haircut. As usual. "It's not my ego that's huge."

They spent the next hour on business. Dallas's new clinic would be up and running in the new year. Construction of the facility, which would be located not far from the air base, had already begun. Ryan's group home was scheduled to open next summer. The bunkhouses were ready.

"My background check is holding up the paperwork," Ryan said, as if they hadn't all known that was likely to happen. He perked up. "I bought ten more Tennessee Walkers, though."

His plans for the group home included getting the kids involved in either horse showmanship or rodeo riding. He claimed he'd chosen the Tennessee Walker for them because William Shatner was a fan, but in reality, he intensely disliked the banned practice of soring—intentionally causing pain to create their famous, high-stepping gait—and in his own way, was trying to improve breeding practices.

This was why Dan had no major concerns as to his motivation for offering to buy off Jazz's family. He was incapable of physical cruelty. Insensitivity, yes. He had that in spades. A giant dose of obliviousness, too. His respect for the law was sometimes a cause for concern, although not so much anymore now that Dan was a sheriff.

But cruelty? Or violence?

Never.

It puzzled him, however, that a man who believed in giving teens second chances had apparently decided Jazz's brothers were a lost cause. To Dan, that was the one thing that didn't make sense.

With business out of the way, the three friends relaxed. Dallas took three beers out of the mini fridge in Ryan's office. They came from the new local brewery. Business for the pretty brew master must be booming.

Dallas passed one beer to Ryan. "Are you still taking pain medication?" he asked Dan, holding his back.

"No. I don't like them." They clouded his thinking.

Dallie handed over his beer. "And yet, you're okay with alcohol."

"I am in small doses." Dan cracked open the can. "What have you guys been up to while I've been glued to the couch?"

"Work," Dallas said. "As usual. How's chasing the hot base manager while nursing a groin injury working out for you?"

"Funny you should ask about Jazz." Dan glanced at Ryan. "She's coming to dinner with my parents tomorrow night. They want to get to know her better. Any comments? Complaints?"

Ryan didn't pretend not to know why he was looking at him. "No complaints here. I like Jazz. But I could save you a fortune if you'd tell her to take me up on my offer. Just sayin'."

"I've missed something," Dallas said, hazel eyes sliding between them before settling on Dan.

"Ryan tried to pay her family to stay away from me."

Dallas slung his arms along the back of the sofa and relaxed into the cushions. "Either one of you could pay mine to stay away from me. I'd love to save a fortune. I'd love to save the suck on my time even more."

"Jazz doesn't want you giving them money," Dan said to Ryan.

Ryan shrugged. "Okay. I'll leave that to you. She didn't tell you about the rest of the conversation though, did she?" He carried on without waiting for an answer. "I suggested she turn the Custer County airport into a full-fledged training base. That would be quite a challenge for her, especially if she wants to give McCall a run for their money. It would be a permanent position, too. She said she'd think about it. So, has she?" He threw that last down like a challenge.

Dan knew where Ryan was going with this. He was reminding him of their conversation in the garage the night of the open house, when he'd warned him Jazz didn't seem all that into him and Dallie suggested she was really looking for a place to belong. If she was into him, and also looking for a place to belong, then turning Custer County into a training base would resolve both of those issues.

Why hadn't she said anything about it to him?

"She was in the middle of an operations plan when I dropped in this afternoon. We didn't have a lot of time to talk." Although she could have found time if she'd had something important to discuss.

Dallas spoke up. "Don't rush things with her, Dan. Let her take the job in McCall and see what happens."

"McCall is twelve hours away." Dan allowed his tone to imply what he thought of the idea.

"We could always let Ryan have that private helicopter he's been begging us for," Dallas said.

"That's a great idea," Ryan chimed in, his eyes lighting up. "It's tax deductible, too."

Except Jazz would be living in Idaho and Dan would be in Montana. Once she accepted that job, nothing would tear her away from it. She took her work seriously—as she should—but he was tired of being patient and taking his chances. Fate could be a real jerk, sometimes. He'd tried letting Andy go and look how that had turned out.

Fate, however, didn't own the whole blame for what had happened to Andy. She'd been thumbing her nose at it for years. At least Jazz didn't have one finger on a self-destruct button. If she needed the job in McCall—if it meant that much to her—then she should take it. They'd find a way to work around it if she did.

He'd talk to her about it after dinner.

✳

HIS MOTHER HAD planned a small barbecue at the ranch.

Dallas had talked Ryan into trying out a virtual reality studio in Forsyth, a neighboring town. After dinner, his parents were off to visit friends for a movie. That would leave Dan with Jazz all to himself, something he really needed.

Except Jazz never showed up. Something had to be wrong because this wasn't like her. The two text messages he sent went unanswered. An hour went by.

"Go ahead and eat or you'll miss your movie," he said to his parents. "I'll drive out to the base and see what's keeping her."

Fifteen minutes later he limped onto the base, cursing the crutches as he fought his way through the heavy exterior door. Inside, he followed the voices. He found six people crowded into the small briefing room. Jazz was hunched over the radio in a world all her own.

Brody, who'd run the obstacle course with him, turned when he entered the room.

"What's going on?" Dan asked him, although by the grim looks on everyone's faces, it wasn't anything good.

"The grassfire in the Swan Range blew up," Brody said. "Larry is missing."

Larry was the youngest and most inexperienced of the smokejumpers on Jazz's team. He and one other man had been dropped onto the western facing slope. Larry then radioed a warning that the wind was unacceptable and not to drop anyone else. He and the smokejumper from Missoula would clear a strip of land and start a controlled burn above the fire line. Unfortunately, the same wind that made it impossible to drop the rest of the team also caused a significant rise in burn conditions. Within twenty-five minutes, the flames were fifteen feet high and traveling upwards at a rate of more than twenty miles per hour. The last message from Larry said that he and his teammate were going to cut downward diagonally on the east side of the fire, according to plan.

"Why didn't anyone call me?" Dan asked.

"Because you're on sick leave, Sheriff. Eli called your office instead."

Jazz started to say something to Eli, standing behind her and peering over her shoulder, and spotted Dan at the back of the room. She signaled for Eli to take her place and pushed through the gathered men to meet Dan by the door. The white script on her beige tank top said *Born to Jump*. She wore matching yoga pants and white canvas flats. Shadowed, anxious blue eyes burdened her delicate face.

Dan followed her out of the briefing room and into the hangar where they could talk in private without disturbing the others. The door shut behind them. Bright light glared from the rafters.

"I'm so sorry. I forgot all about dinner," she said.

He brushed that aside since it was no longer important. He knew exactly how helpless she had to be feeling right now. He'd gone through a similar range of emotions the day he'd been shot and realized his deputy was driving straight into danger.

"How long have the men been missing?" he asked.

"Two hours now. I'm second-guessing myself," she confessed. She jiggled one leg, unable to stand still. "The time of day was all wrong. Most blowups happen before five o'clock. That's why they were dropped in just after five. We last heard from them at five thirty. The operations plan I drafted called for them to get below the fire line and head downhill if it blew up, but it happened so fast. With the wall moving at that speed, there'd be no time for them to reconsider their options. If I made an error, or they were too slow abandoning plan A, they could be dead."

He wished he could hold her and tell her everything would be okay, but she knew the risks far better than he did. "They must have thought the original plan was a good one because they had to agree to it. No one can predict the wind. You've got to trust them, Jazz. They know their jobs or they wouldn't be where they are."

"Right now, I have to decide when to let Larry's parents know he's missing," she said.

He knew how hard that was, too. But it was her job to make the decision, not his. "Are you asking for my advice or are you thinking out loud?"

"Thinking out loud." Her leg continued to jiggle. "I'll wait two more hours. Missoula initially said they wouldn't send firefighters onto the slope after dark, but once the drop in temperature slows the fire down, they said they're sending volunteers with night vision goggles in to check on their last known position."

"What were plans B and C?" They would have talked about possible escape routes before leaving Grand. The two smokejumpers who made it to the ground would have reassessed them after they saw the terrain, too.

"Plan B was to set a controlled burn and clear as large a patch of ground as they could, then crawl into their fire shelters and prepare for a burn-over." Her lower lip trembled into a half smile. "Plan C was the usual. Run like hell."

And in a blowup, the amount of decision-making time available to go from plan A to C was seconds, not minutes. That much, he knew. He understood why she was worried. Larry was young and likely never had to make lifesaving decisions with that speed before. Plus, there was an element of arrogance involved that she'd have to consider. Either one, or both, of those men might have opted to come up with a new plan of their own, which would then cut into those few seconds of reaction time.

"You're on sick leave. You should go home," Jazz said, eyeing the way he was propped on his crutches with concern. "I can call you with an update when I learn more."

He was one more worry she didn't need, but no way was he leaving her. "I'm healing just fine and I'm tired of sitting at home. I'll wait right here with everyone else."

Just after eleven o'clock, they got word that the two

smokejumpers had been found. Both had suffered burns to their hands and faces, and one was banged up from a fall, but they were alive. They'd opted for plan C—they'd dropped their gear and ran like hell, but downhill, as per plan A, through the narrower leading edge of the fire. Then, once they'd reached ground that was already burned, they hunkered down and waited for rescue.

Firefighters were crazy. Dan said as much.

They all laughed at him. "They would have seen the leading edge of the fire from above, before the blowup began, as they parachuted in. That's when they double-check their escape route and why there's an operations plan, so they don't have to waste valuable time making last-minute decisions. Good job on that plan, by the way," Brody congratulated Jazz. "Given the conditions, who'd have thought things would blow up like that?"

Jazz, that was who. Pride for her swelled in Dan's chest.

He ordered pizza for everyone since no one had stopped long enough to eat, and now that the danger was past, they were all hungry.

Jazz went to her office to make that overdue call to Larry's parents. Dan sat on the edge of her desk and listened in. It still wasn't easy, but it was far better than it might have been.

The color had returned to her face by the time the call ended, but he could tell she was wired. His crutches were propped against the wall. She'd turned on a single lamp above her workspace so the light in the office was low.

"Come here," he said once she hung up the phone.

She stepped into the space between his thighs, careful not to bump his injured leg, and into his arms. She rested her forearms on his shoulders, clasping her hands behind his neck, and rested her forehead on his. They were alone, although not entirely. Men called to each other as they moved around in other areas of the hangar, keeping themselves busy while they waited for their pizza to arrive.

"I don't think I can do this," she said quietly.

"We could lock the door. You'll have to try not to scream my name too loud, though. Everyone would know for sure what we're up to then," he said.

Her lips lifted a little. "I don't mean sex. What's wrong with you?"

"I know what you meant." But he'd made her smile, so mission accomplished. He shifted to serious, matching her mood. "Waiting is hard. Not knowing is hard. You'd rather be in the thick of the action. I get it." Whereas he'd far rather be waiting for news on anyone other than on her, although he didn't dare come right out and say it. He'd never asked her how many times she'd been in danger, and he wasn't going to ask, either. He didn't want to know. "You're an excellent base manager, Jazz. You drew on your own experience and training and you didn't make a single mistake. Those guys are alive because they knew what to do when things blew up on them. And because they're crazy."

He had to be crazy too, because if he kept encouraging her this way, she'd take the McCall position for sure.

She pressed her lips to his in a soft, gentle kiss. "Thank you." Her hands went to his face and she kissed him again, deeper, and with a distinct edge of need now.

He skimmed his palms over her hips. While he wasn't averse to having sex in her office, there were too many people around and no lock on the door. They both had careers to think of.

"Want to head back to my place?" he suggested. "Just to get away from here and unwind. It'll be hours before you'll be able to fall asleep. What do you usually do to relax?"

"I usually take my bike out for a ride."

If that was what she needed, then fair enough. Everyone handled stress in their own way. "Why don't I ride with you?"

"You can't ride on the back of a bike with that leg wound."

"We won't know that for a fact until I try, will we?" He cupped her round buttocks. God, they were firm. "It's not as if I'm intentionally going to endanger my parenting potential, if that's what you're afraid of. Your mother's future grandchildren are safe with me."

"Men and their boys..." She rolled her eyes at him. "I thought you were afraid of motorcycles."

He wasn't fond of them, no. But afraid? "Where did you get an idea like that?"

"You're always complaining about them."

"Because I worry about you. I'm not worried about me. I rode dirt bikes when I was a kid. I'm fine."

"Do you ever listen to yourself?" she asked. "Besides, I don't have a spare helmet."

"There's no law in Montana against riding without one."

There was that eyeroll again. "I see how it is with you, Sheriff. You have two sets of rules."

"Only for the people I love."

He said it without thinking. Jazz was the woman he intended to marry, but love was something he'd always equated with Andy—and it had been an exhausting emotion.

Not so with Jazz. It had its challenges, yes. But loving her was like worshipping the sun. It was warm, and constant, and in never-ending supply. She made his heart light when he was with her. And when he wasn't, he had no doubts about her feelings for him. She was as protective of him as she was of her family, who she loved, even if she didn't like them.

But he'd definitely said it too soon. She was too much like Ryan, who'd had to test him by stealing a police car before fully committing to friendship. She didn't understand what love was. She didn't trust him—or anyone—enough to willingly hand them her heart. She'd even taken a clinical approach to their first sexual encounter, although any idiot could tell it wasn't STDs she'd been afraid of.

So how did he make her see that not only did he love her, but she loved him, too?

How did he prove she could trust him?

Chapter Fifteen

JAZZ DIDN'T READ too much into Dan's off-handed declaration of love. Apparently, the girlfriend gag had grown stale enough that he was upping his game in his attempts to distract her, which was sweet, but also annoying, because his timing was terrible. Today had been one of the hardest days of her career and she wasn't in the mood for the joke when she needed a shoulder to lean on. Not just any shoulder, either.

Usually, Dan understood her.

She'd meant it when she said she didn't think she could do this. Being responsible for other people was beyond her capabilities. It was why she'd left Las Vegas and it was why she planned to withdraw her name from the competition for McCall. She was great at looking after herself. She had no problems with being part of a team when the responsibility was shared. But put her in charge of others and her weaknesses all floated straight to the top.

"How would you like to steal a car for a few hours?" Dan asked.

Her brain tried to shift gears. *Enough with the jokes, Dan.*

She should say yes, just to see his reaction.

"I thought you'd put grand theft auto behind you."

The corners of his eyes crinkled. Dark blond eyebrows went up. "I know motorbikes are more your thing, but try and tell me you wouldn't like to take Ryan's Jaguar for a spin."

"I would," she admitted. She could imagine the look on his face. That alone would be worth a few months in jail. "But it's not really stealing if you know he'd lend it to you, and a sedate drive along the Yellowstone at midnight with a law-abiding sheriff sounds mind-numbingly dull, even in a Jag."

"Would it still be dull if the law-abiding sheriff is friends with the owner of the Grand Dragstrip Racetrack, who also happens to owe him a favor?"

He was serious. He was going to let her take one of Ryan's luxury cars to a racetrack. She hugged him. "You're the best."

He wouldn't let her drive his sheriff's SUV to the ranch though, which took away some of the fun, but he gave her the key fob to a brand-new, bright red, Jaguar XE to make up for it.

"If you scratch it, I'll have to buy it for you," he warned her.

She couldn't take her eyes off the sleek car. Her heart was tripping so fast with excitement she thought her chest would explode. "I bet you terrify women when you make threats like that."

"I tailor my threats to the women I'm trying to terrify," he said, popping the passenger side door and easing his injured leg into the seat.

Keeping the Jag under the speed limit on the way to the track was almost too much for her to stand, and if Dan hadn't been with her, she would have opened it up.

The racetrack was a few miles outside of Grand. The owner was waiting to let them in when they arrived at the gate. His name was Roman. He looked like Dwayne Johnson's larger, meaner brother. He whistled as he looked the car over.

"Your buddy must love you," he said to Dan. "This baby has a real engine in her. You aren't driving it on my track without a few rules. Wait here."

He returned a few moments later with a helmet swinging in each hand and a third clenched to his side by the bulge of his arm. "You have to wear these. Dan, you sit in the back. I'm taking shotgun as instructor." He gave Jazz, who was at the wheel, the same onceover he'd given the car, with the same admiring look in his eyes. "Speed limit's one hundred. Maybe more if you can handle the turns." He got in the car and reached for the seat belt. "Buckle up, ladies."

The next hour was the most fun Jazz had had in months. Dan appeared completely relaxed in the back seat as Roman showed her how to heat up the tires, then coached her through turns, gradually allowing her to increase her speed until she passed the one-hundred-mile limit. He called it a night at one hundred and ten.

Dan thanked him as they said goodbye at the gate.

"No problem. She's a natural. Nerves of steel," Roman said. White teeth gleamed as he grinned at Jazz. The weight of one muscled arm strained the cant rail on the roof as he leaned in her window. "Any time you want to come back without him, give me a call and I'll find something for you to drive." He passed her his card.

"Quit hitting on my girlfriend," Dan growled from the passenger seat.

Roman put his hands in the air, laughing. "I don't see no ring on her finger."

"Not yet. It's coming, though," Dan replied.

Jazz was so used to hanging with firefighters she'd known for years and being treated like one of the guys that she'd almost forgotten what it was like to have men over twenty flirting with her. She wouldn't be human if she wasn't flattered. But Dan was the man she was attracted to, and tonight, he'd shown her just how well he knew her. It was scary and exhilarating, and felt much the way driving the Jag at more than one hundred miles per hour had.

He didn't know everything about her, though. For instance, if he made one more joke about her being his girlfriend, she was going to run him down with his friend's car.

They purred along Yellowstone Drive. The streets were

empty. She backed the car into the Endeavour's garage and cut the engine. The headlights winked out on their own and darkness closed in. The inside of the car held the smell of burnt rubber.

"Feel better?" Dan asked.

"I do." She did.

"Ready to talk?"

"That depends," she said warily. "About what?"

"Let's start with McCall."

She ran her fingertip along the top of the steering wheel and tried to sound casual. Matter of fact. "Oh, that. There's not much more to say. I'm going to withdraw my application."

"While I'd love to think it's because you can't live without me and you want to stay in Grand so we can be together, somehow, I doubt that's the reason. So do you mind telling me why?"

Two hours ago, it was because she didn't believe she could handle the stress. Now that she'd gotten past the fear, and her own lack of patience with waiting for news, she wasn't so sure. She'd had time to burn off the adrenaline and accept that her smokejumper was alive, mostly thanks to his own common sense, but also because she'd made sure he was prepared.

What she wasn't yet past was Dan making jokes about their relationship—or lack of one, to be exact.

"Why couldn't that be the real reason?" she demanded,

annoyed.

He had the nerve to look confused. "Why couldn't what be the real reason?"

"Why couldn't it be because I can't live without you and I want to stay in Grand to be with you? Why is the thought of us being a couple such a big joke to you?"

"Now I know for sure that firefighters are crazy," he said. "I've never once suggested our relationship is a joke. We both agreed to be exclusive. You're the one who keeps pointing out to anyone who'll listen that we're not a couple."

"Being exclusive means agreeing not to sleep with other people. It only makes sense. You, on the other hand, told a trash television reporter that I was your girlfriend even before we reached that agreement. It's been a running joke with you ever since."

"It's not a joke. It's me making myself clear. If I'm not serious about you, why would I invite you to have dinner with my parents?"

Now she was the one who was confused. "When were we having dinner with your parents?"

"Who did you think we were having dinner with to-night?"

"I thought it was a party, the same as the open house. You said your mother likes feeding people."

"She does. And tonight, she was planning on feeding you. She and my dad want to get to know you better."

"That's getting too far ahead," Jazz said. A panicky feeling fluttered under her skin.

"Not for me." His voice floated on the car's shadowy interior. "I've loved you since the moment I met you, when you insisted on driving your bike to the base rather than allow me to give you a ride because ten miles was too far to run wearing leather. All I had to do was picture that in my head and I was done for."

The panicky feeling grew worse. "My gene pool suggests I might not be good at making that type of commitment."

"Your genes don't prevent you from being amazing. You'll figure it out. I'll help. You're turning down McCall to be with me, so that's a start. You're making a sacrifice."

"Don't let it go to your head. What's your sacrifice going to be?"

"Are you kidding me? I've met your mother."

And he was still here.

In her head, she knew Dan wouldn't be here with her if he wasn't interested in more. The sex was great. But that wasn't why she was with him, either. Sitting in the dark with him, and talking things through, was even better. Losing this...

That would be hard. Being with him inspired such a broad range of emotions they were hard to sort out, but she did know one thing. It made her happy.

And that made her cautious.

"What if it doesn't work out between us?" she asked.

"We can start off slow. If you really want to take that job

at McCall, then take it. Grand will always be here for you, when—if—you decide you want it."

"Maybe you just think you love me," Jazz said.

She hated that she was this desperate for reassurance, but she had no frame of reference. No one had ever loved her, before. Not since her brothers were little boys, anyway. And she'd let them down, so they could be excused for not loving her anymore.

"I'm positive," he said. "You don't have to say it back. I know it's too soon. All I want is for you to know how I feel, and for you to trust me a little. Not every risk involves jumping out of airplanes and fighting fires, you know. Try taking a chance on having something more in your life than just work."

She did want more. She wanted as much as life had to offer. But she had so much already. Could she afford to be greedy?

"It's not you I don't trust." If he ever decided he'd made a mistake and didn't really love her, she'd survive. She'd learn from it, but she'd be okay. But if she let him down, she'd be hurting him, too. Did she want to be responsible for that? "Maybe we should lay a few ground rules."

"I should have known you'd turn this into a contractual agreement." Humor rolled off him. "Other than the exclusivity clause, which we've already discussed, the only rule I'll agree to is that we talk about any decisions we make that affect our relationship."

A relationship. With Dan. Excitement and fear pulsed through every square inch of her body and threatened to burst through her skin. If she closed her eyes, she was free-falling for the very first time.

But if she was going to do this, she was doing it with her eyes wide open. The best part of the jump was watching the ground race toward her and trying to figure out the right place to land.

"I'm going to pass on McCall." She held up a hand to forestall any comments so she could explain. "Ryan suggested I set up Custer County as another training location. Before I relocate to Grand though, I'm going back to Helena for the winter so I can make plans for next season without anything influencing my judgment. Are you willing to put our relationship on hold until then?"

"Is turning Custer County into a training base what you want?"

"Yes." It turned out Ryan was right. The challenge of building her own base—of training to standards she helped develop—excited her far more than the thought of managing a base other people had already established. She'd never learn to like sending jumpers into danger, but that wasn't bad. It meant she'd always put extra care into her plans.

"I'm sorry, but no. I'm not willing to put our relationship on hold," Dan said, but before her excitement could convert completely to terror, he added, "Because there's no need for it. We've already been talking about buying a private helicopter for the Endeavour and Helena's only about an hour away by air. We'll make it work."

Him having access to that kind of money still boggled her mind. "Perfect. You'll have an airport and a helicopter. I have enough jump hours to qualify as an instructor. Maybe we should start a skydiving school together rather than a smoke-jumping base. Then we could go skydiving when we're stressed instead of stealing Ryan's cars."

"I'm pretty sure you're kidding," he said, "but this might be a good time to say so."

She got out of the car and moved around to the passenger side. She opened his door and sat on his lap, careful not to hurt his injured leg. She draped her arm around his neck. "I promise, if this doesn't work out, it won't be because I didn't try my hardest."

His hand stroked up the length of her spine, then he cupped the back of her head, bringing her lips closer to his. "Are you talking about the base or a long-distance relationship?" he asked.

This level of happiness could only mean one thing.

"Both," she whispered, her heart pounding madly, "because I love you, too."

Epilogue

"LET'S PUT THE sofa there."

Jazz had her hands on her hips and was studying the living room. She didn't have the same fear of redecorating that had paralyzed Dan. The ugly artwork was gone.

He was glad she'd decided not to pursue the position at McCall. But it was only after a year of back-and-forth travel between Grand and her firefighter position in Helena that she'd finally agreed to move in with him.

The cohabitation agreement she'd insisted on signing hadn't been necessary. Yes, her family had approached him for money. On multiple occasions. But he'd had even less trouble saying no to them than she had with redecorating the house. If they were any good at extortion they wouldn't have been living in poverty for as long as they had.

He'd insisted on buying a house for her mother, however. In Las Vegas, of course. He wasn't moving her to the ranch, as she'd wanted. Her house was in his name and the bills came to him. At least Jazz knew she'd have a roof over her head and food in the fridge. After that, she was on her own. Her brothers were another matter entirely. He'd met with them—Jazz didn't know—and they would get nothing from him. He'd sat her down and told her if she wanted to give them money then that was up to her, but he was having no part of it. It was time she focused less on how disappointed she believed they were in her and more on how they hadn't taken better control of their own lives. She wasn't their mother.

Right now, he had a ring burning a hole in his pocket. He'd chosen a blue sapphire, the same color as her eyes. It wasn't anything close to ostentatious. He knew all too well her opinion on flashing money around. He planned on giving it to her before the victory party tonight. If she thought her family might hurt his chances for reelection—which they hadn't—wait until she discovered their take on the sheriff living in sin.

Finding the right time, however, was proving more difficult than expected. His mother and sisters were here, taking care of the kitchen preparations, because it turned out Jazz was a terrible cook. Even worse than he was. Beyond toast and fresh fruit, they were a lost cause. Dallie and Ryan had been in and out all morning too, helping them rearrange furniture.

"Let's dump all this for a few hours and go for a ride," he suggested. She'd taken to ranch life like a duck to water and riding was one of her favorite things.

The air was cool. It was early spring, and the ice was

barely gone from the river. The yellowed fields hadn't yet shed their tangled winter coats.

Dan turned the horses toward the swimming hole. "I have something I want to show you," he said.

"I've seen it, and you can forget it. I fell for that bathwater trick once before." The raw wind nipped the tip of her nose, turning it pink. "We could always slip into the barn on the way back, though. It'll be a while before anyone looks for us."

He laughed. And that was why he loved her. She had a great sense of humor. It had taken her months to truly become comfortable in their relationship, but now that she was, he loved her even more. When she made a commitment, she was all in.

"This won't take long."

"It never does."

"Them's fighting words, ma'am." He slid from the saddle and gazed up at her on her horse. "Marry me, Jazz." He reached into his pocket and pulled out the ring. He placed his hands over her left one grasping the reins. He eased the ring onto her finger.

She stared at it for long moments. It sparkled bright blue in the sunlight. He was pretty confident of her feelings, but she was taking way too long to say something, right now. Always, when she was speechless, he'd learned to look in her eyes. It was why he'd bought her a ring to match.

She looked down at him. Happiness spilled from her eyes. She slid out of the saddle and into his waiting arms.

"I love you," she said, and he kissed her.

The End

Want more? Pre-order the next book in the Grand, Montana series, *The Montana Doctor*!

Join Tule Publishing's newsletter for more great reads and weekly deals!

If you enjoyed *The Montana Sheriff*,
you'll love the next books in…

The Grand, Montana series

Book 1: *The Montana Sheriff*

Book 2: *The Montana Doctor*
Coming in April 2022!

Book 3: *The Montana Rancher*
Coming in June 2022!

Available now at your favorite online retailer!

More books by Paula Altenburg

The Montana McGregor Brothers series

Book 1: *The Rancher Takes a Family*

Book 2: *The Rancher's Secret Love*

Book 3: *The Rancher's Proposal*

A Sweetheart Brand series

Book 1: *Her Montana Brand*

Book 2: *The Cowboy's Brand*

Book 3: *Branded by the Cowboy*

Available now at your favorite online retailer!

About the Author

USA Today Bestselling Author Paula Altenburg lives in rural Nova Scotia, Canada with her husband and two sons. A former aviation and aerospace professional, Paula now writes contemporary romance and fantasy with romantic elements.

Thank you for reading

The Montana Sheriff

If you enjoyed this book, you can find more from all our great authors at TulePublishing.com, or from your favorite online retailer.

TULE
PUBLISHING

CPSIA information can be obtained
at www.ICGtesting.com
Printed in the USA
LVHW030311030222
709976LV00004B/290

9 781954 894730